The Darkest Destiny

Sign up for the 1001 Dark Nights Newsletter
and be entered to win a Tiffany Key necklace.

There's a contest every month!

Go to www.1001DarkNights.com to subscribe.

**As a bonus, all subscribers can download
FIVE FREE exclusive books!**

Acknowledgments from the Author

A huge thank you and hug to ladies I love but also adore: Jill Monroe, Naomi Lane, Liz Berry, Jillian Stein and MJ Rose.

One Thousand and One Dark Nights

Once upon a time, in the future…

*I was a student fascinated with stories and learning.
I studied philosophy, poetry, history, the occult, and
the art and science of love and magic. I had a vast
library at my father's home and collected thousands
of volumes of fantastic tales.*

*I learned all about ancient races and bygone
times. About myths and legends and dreams of all
people through the millennium. And the more I read
the stronger my imagination grew until I discovered
that I was able to travel into the stories… to actually
become part of them.*

*I wish I could say that I listened to my teacher
and respected my gift, as I ought to have. If I had, I
would not be telling you this tale now.
But I was foolhardy and confused, showing off
with bravery.*

*One afternoon, curious about the myth of the
Arabian Nights, I traveled back to ancient Persia to
see for myself if it was true that every day Shahryar
(Persian: شهریار, "king") married a new virgin, and then
sent yesterday's wife to be beheaded. It was written
and I had read that by the time he met Scheherazade,
the vizier's daughter, he'd killed one thousand
women.*

Something went wrong with my efforts. I arrived in the midst of the story and somehow exchanged places with Scheherazade — a phenomena that had never occurred before and that still to this day, I cannot explain.

Now I am trapped in that ancient past. I have taken on Scheherazade's life and the only way I can protect myself and stay alive is to do what she did to protect herself and stay alive.

Every night the King calls for me and listens as I spin tales. And when the evening ends and dawn breaks, I stop at a point that leaves him breathless and yearning for more. And so the King spares my life for one more day, so that he might hear the rest of my dark tale.

As soon as I finish a story... I begin a new one... like the one that you, dear reader, have before you now.

Prologue

Brochan the Undeterred scanned the immortal nightclub and scowled. *Too many people. Music is too loud. Strobe lights are too bright. Scents too cloying.* He hated this place. Granted, he hated most places.

At the moment, he perched alone at a shadowed table. Alone, always his preference. No one proved foolish enough to approach him. He'd left Nevaeh, the uppermost sky realm accessible only to Sent Ones, and entered the lower sky realms accessible to all, thinking to observe his younger brother. A boy he'd raised as a son for hundreds of years after their parents deemed the troubled, three-year-old McCadden "demon tainted" in order to relinquish all responsibility for him. Considering Brochan and McCadden were born and bred demon assassins, the label came with problems.

Though only fifteen back then, Brochan had moved out and overseen the child's care himself. The second he'd beheld the tiny, squalling infant, he'd known love for the first time. True love based on a decision more than a feeling. A willing determination to protect the boy with his life, no matter what he thought or what he felt. No matter the cost.

For the bulk of his existence, Brochan had lived for his child's happiness. At the age of eighteen, he'd even petitioned the High Council for a wife, eager to give the lad a mother.

The Council had agreed and selected a Messenger named Samantha. With high hopes, Brochan wed the quiet maid. But after only three years, she ended the joyless union and left him, never looking back.

Her departure had broken McCadden's heart just as fiercely as their parents' desertion. In desperation, Brochan had wed a second female, Rebecca.

She left him two years later.

What should have been a mild inconvenience for Brochan nearly destroyed the boy. Another tragic heartbreak to endure. After that, he'd made a vow. He and McCadden to the end, and *only* he and McCadden. The two of them and no other.

So why had the formerly ready-to-laugh-at-anything soldier acted so strange lately? Constantly lost in thought. Somber. His smiles, his merriment erased without a trace remaining. His teasing nature? Suddenly nonexistent. Something bothered the lad greatly, but what? Why wouldn't he admit it? Throughout their centuries together, Brochan had never offered judgment, only solutions.

Even now, the dim lighting around the bar couldn't hide McCadden's misery. The black walls and surrounding mob of merry drinkers merely highlighted it.

A commotion drew Brochan's gaze to the left, where immortals of every species were backing away, creating a path. A female strode down it, coming into view, and his jaw dropped.

Propelled by a force greater than himself, he leaped to his feet. His massive white and gold wings snapped into his sides, the hem of his ivory robe falling over his sandaled feet. She approached…him?

He lost his breath, his heart thudding. Had he ever seen such an exquisite sight?

A thick mane of pale waves framed the most arresting face in existence—a delicate tapestry of perfection. Flawless golden skin, vivid umber eyes and scarlet lips offered a collage of colors. She wore a short, barely-there dress of the finest ice-blue silk that molded to lush curves.

Questions filled his head. *Who is she? And how soon can I grab her?*

The blood heated in his veins, burning hotter and hotter. Boiling! Sweat beaded on his brow. His heart thudded with more force. Enough to crack a rib. Or perhaps the pangs erupted because of another reason? How was he to know anything about anything right now? He'd never felt a sensation quite like this.

The female sauntered closer, soon to be within his reach. Every fiber of his being stood at attention and shouted, *MINE! My mate.*

Mate? His? A partner? The one led by fate to enrich his life.

He readjusted his vow. It would be Brochan, his brother and this female to the end. The three of them. He'd never thought to possess a mine. But her… *I will possess. Woe to anyone who thinks to take her from me!*

He braced, ready to pounce. To seize his prize. The need to touch her proved nigh irresistible. Here, now, he could admit the truth. Deep down, he'd wanted a mine more than he'd ever wanted anything.

Did she feel a similar pull? She must. The way she was looking at him…as if she'd never glimpsed a more glorious sight.

His chest puffed with pride. He wasn't a handsome male. A fact he'd never lamented until now. But no matter. In battle, he fought with ruthless precision. What's more, he kept himself strong, packing his body with strength. No one would defend her better than Brochan.

As she entered his orbit, the sweetest scent hit his nostrils. His head fogged. For a moment, he couldn't move—he could only inhale for more.

Her lips curved into a soft smile just before she strolled past him. He balled his hands into fists. He didn't understand what just happened. Surely she felt *something* for him. He couldn't be alone in this too. The feeling was far too power— What was she doing?

He sucked in a breath. She seemed to home in on…McCadden? The lad observed her with the most intense desire he'd ever displayed.

No. This couldn't be transpiring.

But it was.

Shock nailed Brochan in place as the two sized each other up. Horror followed, inundating him. His woman and his brother…a couple? No. Fate would not be so cruel.

He crumpled into his seat, the abrupt motion ripping feathers from his wings. Golden down floated around him as he watched McCadden smile…watched as hours ticked past and she roused laugh after laugh from the lad.

From there, the two rarely parted. In less than a week, she won his brother's stalwart declaration of love.

Brochan observed the blossoming love match from the shadows, always in the shadows, aching, cursing his lust for the female. Her name was Viola the Incomparable, and she was a goddess of the Afterlife. She treated a pet devil-dog like an infant and complimented herself regularly, constantly drawing a smile to Brochan's lips as much as McCadden's.

Cease yearning for her? Impossible. Resist her, however? Yes. Always. How could he do any less? She alone had prompted his brother's recovery.

Today, Brochan kept his distance from the couple. He kept his distance from *everyone*, his temper at an all-time high. He paced the confines of his home, a cloud in Nevaeh, the uppermost sky realm where he kept everything just the way he liked it: minimal, his only furnishings a bed and a desk. McCadden and Viola were currently on a special *date*. To consummate their relationship? Brochan's stomach twisted.

A loud boom. A heavy thump. He straightened, on instinct extending an arm. A sword of fire appeared in his grip. The front door? He flashed there. McCadden! His brother crawled inside the home, blood smeared across his face and wetting his once-white robe. And his wings...

They'd begun to wither.

Dread surged. Withering wings meant only one thing... A mortal death loomed.

Not him! Brochan lifted the lad as gently as possible and carried him to the bed. Someone would suffer for this! *Today.* "What happened? What of Viola?" Panic struck, quickly consuming him. "Where is she?" Was she hurt? Did she still live?

The moisture in his mouth dried. *Not her!*

McCadden averted his gaze, tears sliding down his cheeks. "She did this, brother. She took my immortality. Fed it to her pet and left me to die."

That...no. She wouldn't do that. She wouldn't condemn Brochan's only family to death. She wouldn't force him to punish a female he only longed to protect. "Are you certain?" He scrubbed a hand over his mouth. "Perhaps you misremember what—"

"I misremember nothing!" McCadden spat the words before rolling to his side. The necrosis continued to spread through his wings, white and gold feathers blackening. "She never cared about me. She used me."

Righteous fury pulsed from his brother, illuminating the sincerity of every word. Reality settled in, replacing his shock. The goddess *had* done this. The mate of Brochan's dreams had *dared.*

Claws grew from his nailbeds, sharper than ever before. She had harmed his brother in the worst way. Therefore, she couldn't be his mate. He'd been mistaken about that. Protect her? Not now, not ever. She would pay for her crime. He would see to it personally.

A life for a life.

Without wings—the source of his power and his only key into the realm—McCadden couldn't remain in Nevaeh. He would become a Fallen One. An enemy.

In that moment, Brochan knew two things. He would not remain without his brother. So he must fall.

Bitterness was forbidden to Sent Ones. With good reason! It acted as a terrible poison. A highly contagious sickness with only one cure: forgiveness. Without that forgiveness, Brochan's wings would wither into nothing, just like his brother's. *If* he managed to avoid detection long enough for the process to complete. As soon as another Sent One sniffed out the animosity he smuggled in his heart, he would face immediate exile and the forced removal of his wings.

He hardened his heart. Forgive Viola? No. He'd barely managed the feat with his parents and his wives.

A burn flourished in his chest, intensifying swiftly, and he blinked. Did bitterness already attempt to burrow and root?

Better to leave Nevaeh now. If he waited for an official eviction, his wings would be removed by blade rather than time. To mete his revenge against the goddess, he required his wings as long as possible.

"Worry not, brother. I will see to the goddess," he vowed. "She will pay for this. And I will find a way to save you. Nothing will stop me."

Chapter One

Glorious. Wondrous. Incomparable. Viola, goddess of the Afterlife, drank in the sight before her. The beauty! Had she ever viewed such a flawless masterpiece? Such perfect perfection? Dazed, she tilted her head left, right, down, up, studying the image from different angles. *Only gets better.*

The dips and rises. The subtle shading of colors. Layer upon layer of exquisite detail. Honestly, *nothing* compared to this. The sheer, unadulterated majesty welled tears in her eyes.

From somewhere nearby, a man asked, "Is she admiring...herself?"

"She is," another man replied, glee in the undertone. "She's possessed by the demon of Narcissism. To capture her, I had only to hold up this mirror. Within seconds, she stopped fighting."

The duo laughed, pleased with themselves.

Silly males. She wasn't possessed, a term used too loosely among their ilk. She was *oppressed*. There was a big difference. *Possession* equaled a total takeover. *Oppression* pointed to shackles of influence the fiend utilized liberally, all from the safety of a stronghold it had built inside her mind. A stronghold she had *allowed* it to build.

Ignorance destroyed as surely as a blade.

Now, Narcissism sought adoration and destruction in equal measure, and used her to get it.

Someone applied pressure to her shoulders, forcing her to perch on an uncomfortable chair. Oh, wow. *And I thought such perfection couldn't be improved.* Standing, she was magnificent. But sitting? More so.

One of her companions drew her arms behind her back. Something cold and hard circled her wrists. The same sensations registered on her ankles as well. Fetters?

I look amazing in chains.

No, no. This isn't right.

"Remove her weapons," the second male commanded.

In a shadowy corner of Viola's mind, she knew she'd allowed this detainment for a specific purpose. She remembered waking to the sound of her alarm clock—clapping and cheering, as she deserved. Then she had beautified—aka breathed—and gone to a bar to condemn someone to death and...what, what? Just as soon as she broke the mirror's spell, she would remember her endgame, then save herself and the day. Obviously. There was no one as strong or wise as her. But...

Shouldn't she admire her sun-kissed skin a little longer? What about the mischievous glint in her rich umber eyes? The classic perfection of her bone structure. The waterfall of silken blond locks. The delicacy of her—

A dark cloth whooshed over the glass, hiding her reflection.

Narcissism clawed in protest. His specialty.

As sharp pains ripped through her head, she bellowed, "I'll strangle you with your entrails!" Viola erupted from the chair, planning to do just that. Nope. The fetters held steady, locking her in place.

Realization dawned. *I'm trapped?* Panic warred with rage. She didn't accept captivity well. The daughter of a powerful goddess, Viola had spent the first twenty-six years of her life trapped inside a palace, hidden by her mother from the woman's more powerful spouse. Hidden from all the worlds. It had been an opulent home, yes, but a prison all the same.

Not long after her escape, she was arrested by an *army* of gods. She ended up spending a multitude of centuries sealed inside the impenetrable Tartarus, a jailhouse for immortals. Worse, until recently, she'd thought *herself* responsible for her incarceration. That she had done something horribly wrong and ended the wrong soul at the wrong time. In reality, the demon had hidden the truth from her, and it was something far worse than she could have ever imagined. A truth devastating to her sense of self-worth.

Well, never again! Not the lower than dirt self-esteem and certainly not the lock-up.

The demon continued its assault, and oh, how she despised the foul, horrid creature. Demons brimmed with evil and oozed wickedness. They had no redeeming qualities and couldn't be reasoned with. Couldn't be satisfied or placated. Insidious, each of them, with a single purpose: cause as much pain and destruction as possible. For their hosts. For those their hosts loved.

At first, she hadn't even noticed the fiend's presence. Then, it had begun to whisper to her. She'd foolishly listened, allowing her new companion to provoke certain emotions. Indignation. Offense. Envy. More whispers had come. The more she'd mused on its words, the stronger her emotions became, soon creating a bond between them, making her a slave to the wiles of her greatest enemy. In the aftermath, the person she used to be—the person she *should* be—had gotten lost.

Focus. Think. The past didn't matter. Viola settled into the seat. Inhale. Exhale. As awareness of the present situation returned, she took stock. A small room. No, a cell. Dank and dirty with a mud floor and crumbling, blood-stained brickwork. An array of torches hung on the walls, providing light without heat. The frigid air was putrid and infused with the scent of rot.

From a legendary vampire bar to a crappy dungeon? The insult! An exquisite female like Viola deserved wining and dining in pure luxury, nothing less.

The only other occupants: her kidnappers, the speakers. Two Fallen Ones with wings. Former Sent Ones. Only, their wings hadn't rotted off, an act that would have stripped them of their immortality and all its boons. How certain individuals retained their wings, she didn't know. But the rare few who did…changed.

These two had undergone a transformation, and the result wasn't pretty.

They stood across the cell, near the bars, clad in only loose-fitting pants. The tallest had leathery, crimson skin. The other sported green flesh speckled with onyx. Both had too-prominent facial features and cesspool irises. Black wings with razor-sharp edges arched over broad shoulders. Curling claws tipped their hands and feet.

What did these males want with her? Other than the obvious, of course.

Viola exaggerated a sigh. "Listen, boys. You're not the first misguided souls to abduct me, hoping to level up and win the most beautiful goddess ever born. Like every time before, my answer is no. I absolutely will not agree to be your captive bride, bear your Fallen spawn, and make you the happiest of creatures. Although, you *do* have an almost delicious muscle mass, so what the heck? A little role-playing might not be amiss. Try not to get offended when I moan someone else's name."

Crimson shuddered, then offered her a chiding look. "I decline with every fiber of my being. I prefer my females to be…not you."

"Okay. Sure." She rolled her eyes. "Whatever you need to tell yourself." Everyone desired her. How could they not? Forget her stunning beauty and brilliant mind. If possible. She had so many magnificent qualities. So much more to offer. Her sparkling wit and magical laugh delighted all who heard her—and also those who didn't. Intelligent beyond words, she'd even helped her own mother birth her. And Viola had done most of the work! Forget Helen of Troy. Viola had launched *two* thousand ships with a wink.

Ignore the pang of uncertainty in your chest. It means nothing.

"Your ultimate fate isn't in question, goddess," the Fallen One announced. "Be assured, you *will* die today. But there's no reason for you to fret about it. Answer my questions, and I'll end you swiftly."

Poor, addled soul. He believed he had the necessary power to defeat her. *Her!* Should she laugh now or later?

Wait. Why not now *and* later?

Viola laughed, and it was more magical than advertised. "A swift end sounds boring."

He shrugged. "That is your choice. Just understand I still plan to kill you. But this way, I'll ensure you linger."

"Ohhhh. Yes, let's do that." She nodded for emphasis. "I love dramatic goodbyes. No, you know what? I think I'll escape my bonds and murder *you* instead. Yes, I'll do that. But there's no reason to fret about it," she added, gifting him with a blinding smile. "I'll make it hurt no matter what you do."

Confusion registered, contorting each male's features as they shared a look. One shrugged, then the other. Then fury took hold, currents rippling through their wings.

"Apparently, you haven't comprehended the gravity of your situation," Crimson said. "Allow me to help the light dawn. The shackles prevent you from flashing, misting, or disembodying in any way. Escape is impossible for you. You are at my mercy, and I have little to spare."

So the fetters prevented her best tricks. So what? A downer but certainly not a deterrent. So her captors had stripped her of swords, daggers, poisons and a crossbow. Again, so what? They hadn't bothered to remove her array of jewelry. The most dangerous weapons of all.

Buffoons! Few expected a goddess as magnificent as Viola to excel in weaponry. But, when you had a childhood as lonely as hers, with no one to rely on, you learned to protect yourself in creative ways.

"Let's begin our chat, shall we?" Crimson dragged a metal chair in front of hers, his flexing muscles on display. Careful of his wings, he eased down. All the while, his buddy Gangrene paced behind him.

She could guess what they wished to discuss. For months, a third Fallen One with blue skin and silver eyes had tracked her from realm to realm. His name was Brochan, and he was a monster. A true beast. Though he only ever revealed himself to her for two reasons: When danger surrounded her, or when she hunted prey for Fluffy, her beloved soulmate. A Tasmanian devil slash vampire—or rather, devampire.

Fluffy had saved her life on more than one occasion. Literally! He was a better person than most people. Loyal, brave, unwavering no matter the goal. How many others could say the same?

Foolish Brochan had developed a routine. Materialize, save the day if needed, then point to her and intone, "Forsaken" before vanishing. He did no more and no less. Despite his denunciation, he never harmed her or allowed others to do so.

Clearly, he'd fallen in love with her and had no idea how to express his feelings properly. Surprise, surprise. *Join the club, big boy.*

How Brochan must hate himself for his (understandable) weakness. He desperately hungered for the female who'd stolen his brother's lifeforce. The eternal battery.

In her defense, she did what she wanted, when she wanted, without fail. It was like science or something. Although, yes, her actions had condemned the Sent One—McCadden—to a mortal death.

Did she feel guilt and regret? Of course. But also, no. Mostly no. Everything she did, she did for Fluffy's wellbeing. What was there to regret?

There was no line she wouldn't cross for the little darling. Fluffy had never lied to her. His growls and buzzing noises always proclaimed the truth. He'd never betrayed her or abandoned her, either. Had never bitterly resented her, smiling on the outside while dying of jealousy inside.

What was Brochan's problem, anyway? It wasn't like McCadden had gifted her with top-of-the-line immortality or anything. Scarcely a year had passed since she'd fed it to Fluffy, yet her adorable devampire already required another meal.

Viola's stomach twisted as thoughts of his demise tormented her. Again and again, Brochan had ruined her efforts to procure any sustenance. How many more months—weeks?—could her baby last?

Can't lose him. So. Her path was clear. Brochan must die. No one endangered her precious and lived to tell the tale. In fact, Viola already considered Brochan a dead man. Now, she had only to decide on the means.

There were two possible paths to travel. Road A: Question her abductors to discover Brochan's greatest weaknesses, then murder them all. Road B: Stall until Brochan showed up, let him murder his brethren on her behalf, then turn around and murder *him*.

Good news was, both ways ended in success for her.

If only she could feed these males to Fluffy. But winged Fallen Ones were poison to all other species. Their blood killed vampires, while their souls extinguished phantoms and other spirit beings.

"Goddess," Crimson snapped. "Are you listening to me?"

"No," she admitted. "Pro-tip. If you want my attention, be more interesting. Bonus points if you're even a *little* handsome. In case no one ever told you, you could be almost okay-looking...if you change everything about yourself."

His eyes blazed with fiery emotion. Admiration, no doubt. A common occurrence for Viola. He grated, "Why does Brochan protect someone as despicable as you?"

"Despicable?" Narcissism snarled, fury infiltrating every crevice of her mind. The demon demanded adoration, fuel, at all times. Without it, the fiend turned on *her*, ceasing to hide the worst of her memories, unleashing a river of frothing self-hatred.

Oh, yes. Beneath the surface of Viola's well deserved and perfectly inflated pride, seethed an ocean of self-loathing. *Unlovable! Unwanted! So easily forgotten!*

Once she had suffered enough, Narcissism built her back up and started the process over again. Love, hatred. Love, hatred. A vicious tug-of-war she won and lost simultaneously. A horrendous cycle she'd grown to both despise and appreciate. Before this, she'd had no self-love at all.

Every so often, she caught flashes of those dreaded memories, buried so deeply. In each, she was smiling and talking. Which she didn't understand. How could that type of remembrance hurt her? And yet, deep down, she knew utter devastation awaited her. It always did.

Crimson snapped his fingers in front of her face, pulling her from the dark mire of her musings. "I asked you a question, goddess."

He had? Oh, yes. "You asked why Brochan is so full of awe for me. A question with an obvious answer. But go ahead and tell me your theories. I'll let you know if you're right or not."

Crimson's eyes turned to slits. "Brochan is a male with a single purpose. The salvation of his brother. Nothing and no one can stop him from pursuing his goal—except you. Why?"

"He loves and adores me. Why else?" Viola had done her due diligence and asked around. Rumors suggested her monstrous stalker had been a highly decorated Sent One, with more demon kills than any other. "If he blamed me, he would have attempted to kill me at least once."

"Brochan will never desire his brother's killer," Crimson said. "He despises you with the whole of his being. Try again."

Despised *her*? Viola winced, so sorry for this oblivious creature. "Wow. This is awkward. One of us is dead wrong, and it's clear to everyone in the room it's you. How embarrassed you must be."

Crimson came up out of his chair and slapped her. Pain exploded through her cheek, the blow packing enough power to whip her head to the side. As she straightened, blood leaked from the corner of her mouth.

Calm. Steady. She breathed deeply, her heartbeat harmonizing with the click-clack of Gangrene's claws as he paced at a faster clip. When Viola's temper got the better of her, she shifted into a horrifying combination of Narcissism and...something else. Her other half.

She cringed. The most wretched abomination in all the lands...a common feline shifter.

Oh, how she burned with humiliation at the thought! Why had her mother cheated with a common alley cat? Why couldn't *that* fact remain hidden from Viola?

"Do I have your attention?" Crimson asked, getting more comfortable in his seat. "You requested my theory. Well, here it is. When Brochan isn't chasing you, he's questioning others about you and a key to Nevaeh. I suspect you own one, and Brochan intends to steal it. So. What do you think? Is my theory correct?"

"Are you referring to the rumor started by me—I mean, *someone other than me*—claiming my body is a key to Nevaeh? Because it is."

"Give me the key, goddess." Crimson stated the words with enough fire to burn down an entire planet.

"Since you asked politely...no, thanks."

He bared his fangs at her. "Give me. The key. Or you *will* suffer."

"Oh, good gracious," she said, simpering at him. "I'm so sorry. I didn't realize you were serious until just now. Sure, I'll give you the key. I hid it in one of my fingers. Free the cuffs, and I'll show you."

He swung at her, his palm meeting her cheek for a second time. Her head whipped to the side with more force, her body jerking, pulling the shackles tight. The sharp sting set off a high-pitched ringing in her ears.

When she settled, she smiled at him. In a sing-song voice, she said, "You're going to die screaming."

"Enough!" Gangrene strode over and punched her with a balled fist. "Give us the key!"

This time, her brain butted up against her skull, searing agony radiating across her jaw. Dizziness swept in, and nausea surged as blood soaked her tongue. Did she back down? Not even a little. She spit at Gangrene, delighting as scarlet rained over his features.

He geared to strike her again, only to pause when electricity charged the air. A strange, wild wind blew in, snuffing out a torch with a soft *pfft*. Viola sat up straighter. Brochan?

First, excitement swept over her. *Can't stay away. Wants me too intently.* All too soon, trepidation crept down her spine. What if she had maybe, possibly, perhaps…misread his feelings for her and the Fallen were right? What if Brochan despised her?

Not everyone was smart enough to realize her amazingness. If Brochan did hate her, he might attack the moment he learned the truth about that nonexistent key. A ludicrous idea, yes, but sometimes she must entertain even the most farfetched notions to discover a truth.

As Viola worked stealthily to unfasten the metal binding her wrists—yes! success!—she maintained a composed façade on the outside. "If Brochan plans to steal my key, as you suggest, he'll do everything in his power to rescue me, yes? Even slaughter his kinsmen. Do you think he's here now?"

Crimson ran a forked tongue over an incisor. A revealing tell. He feared Brochan *greatly*. "Go up. Ensure we remain alone," he told Gangrene, who flashed seconds later, vanishing from view. Scowling at her, Crimson grated, "Want to keep your pretty face? Reveal where you've hidden the key."

"Pretty face? I *knew* you desired me. Lust is practically seeping out of your pores."

Growling now, he unsheathed a serrated blade. "I'll start with your tongue. It's coming out, one way or another."

A strange noise quieted him—a heavy thud and roll. In unison, Viola and Crimson glanced to the side, watching as Gangrene's head trundled into the cell—without his body.

Brochan *was* here.

She jolted, the urge to free her ankles and flash to the nearest safe house too strong to disregard. For Fluffy, she found the courage to resist. A good scheme always cost a bit of sanity. She'd put a plan into motion, and she would see it through.

Crimson leaped, flaring his wings and bracing to attack. Too late. Brochan materialized a few feet away, a seven-foot tower of pure strength, his claws long, sharp and already arching through the air. Her captor's head flew to the ground, joining Gangrene's. Blood spurted as the rest of him toppled.

Mouth drying, Viola peered up at the male who'd tracked her for so long. *Such power.* Sometimes, he struck her as monstrous. Other times, magnificent. Today, he was somehow both at once, and she kind of, sort of...liked it. Black horns had grown from his skull, curling backward with sharp tips pointing down. His forehead seemed more prominent than before. His cheeks and chin, too. Broad shoulders led to well-defined pecs and row after row of strength. Blue skin now possessed swirling designs that ran the length of his arms and over his hands. Claws grew from his fingertips *and* toes. And how cute was that?

She frowned. He had no right to showcase such smoldering sex appeal at a time like this. She had too much work to do, and distractions wouldn't be tolerated.

Viola exhaled with determination. *Must play this cool.* "Um, Brochan? Hi. It's me, the glorious object of your greatest obsession."

Looking as if he'd just returned from a century-long bender of steroids, testosterone and undiluted evil, he shifted his blazing silver gaze to her and raised an arm, pointing.

"I'm Forsaken," she said before he had a chance to speak. "Yes, I know. Be a dear and release me?" She batted her lashes, doing her best to appear distressed. "I'm so vulnerable...in such terrible danger, and I'm willing to bargain for my safety. I'll trade anything. Surely, I have something you want? Your friends mentioned a key. I have so many. What do I care about parting with one?"

He remained in place, unmoving, not seeming to breathe. Deciding whether to kill her now or offer aid as he'd done in the past?

Either way, he died today. He was a danger to Fluffy—and to Viola.

"If you wish to aid me without receiving compensation, that's fine, too," she continued, playing her role to perfection. Meanwhile, she slid the metal bracelet from her wrist and gripped one end. She wouldn't feel bad about Brochan's demise. Not even a little. "Although, my happiness is probably the best compensation in town."

He stared at her intently, as if determined to peer into her soul.

"Why have you aided me in the past, anyway?" she asked. Why not take advantage of this prime opportunity? "What do you plan to do with me?"

Minutes passed. He didn't move a muscle. Finally, he spoke. "You'll know what I decide to do with you as soon as I do."

The most words he'd ever uttered to her. And in such a guttural voice. Wow! The tones and nuances washed over her, drawing white-hot goose bumps to the surface of her skin. Then he stomped over…

My plan is working? Of course, my plan is working. I'm brilliant!

The beginnings of her grin peeked out when Brochan leaned down to undo her manacles. Without hesitation, she swung her arm. Target? His throat. With her movement, the bracelet unfolded section by section, locking into a long, thin sword. *Whoosh.*

Like Gangrene and Crimson before him, Brochan lost his head. Shock etched into every feature. His body crashed to the floor.

"Sorry, but I went ahead and decided what you'll do to and with me," she told his bleeding corpse as she liberated her ankles. "You'll be doing *nothing*. Enjoy."

Unfettered at last, she stood. Swiping her hands together in a job well done, she stepped over each Fallen One and strolled away without looking back. Now, to finally see to her darling.

Chapter Two

Brochan opened his eyes amid a chorus of cursing, courtesy of the other two Forsaken who'd lost their heads this day. Reality crystalized. *Killed again.* By *her* hand. This was his fourth death, each one caused by the goddess in some way. Not that she knew it. This was the first time she'd overseen the deed personally, using a breathy plea and a razor-sharp blade he hadn't seen coming.

Even as he lamented her very existence, he admired her creativity and cunning. Her beauty and charm. But then, his reactions to her had always swung from one extreme to another. From longing to resentment, disdain to desire, mercilessness to tenderness.

Hate her.

Crave her.

No doubt she believed she had slain Brochan for good. Soon, however, she would learn better. Fallen Ones like Brochan, Midian, and Joseph—those known as the Forsaken—were deathless. No injury, not even a beheading, kept them down for long.

After a demise, any demise, their minds flicked off for a short period, and their bodies transformed in some way. The first time, Brochan's bronze skin had turned blue. The second, his navy eyes had lightened to silver. Then the feathers had fallen out of his wings. Horns had grown. What horrifying change awaited him today?

He scanned the scene of his newest resurrection. His head had yet to rejoin with his body. Same for Midian and Joseph. There was no sign of Viola, though her sweet rose scent lingered inside his nostrils.

Midian—a Forsaken with red skin and too much rage—snarled, "The goddess arranged your brother's expiration date, and you opt to aid her over us, your comrades? Fool! We merely seek a key to Nevaeh. One we will share with you."

"The goddess is mine," Brochan snarled back. "Her pain and end are mine to mete. *Only* mine." At some point, Brochan would strike at her. Until then, he must do everything necessary to ensure his hatred won the battle against his desires. "No one else is to touch her."

He'd never hungered for anyone the way he still hungered for Viola. Had never yearned for *anything* this intensely.

How did he make it stop?

"You don't seek the key," Midian gasped. "You want *her*, just as she boasted."

Declare his weakness for the goddess to another? Never! "I seek my vengeance, and I expect—*demand*—a clear path."

Once, he and Midian had served together in the Sent One army. They'd fought side by side, battle after battle. The moment the male dared to bruise Viola, he had ended whatever remained of their friendship.

Suddenly, Joseph's head went skidding across the cell, past the metal bars and down the hall as if yanked by an invisible string, mystically drawn to the headless body Brochan had left in a corridor above.

Midian's body vibrated soon after, his head sliding over, closing in to begin the process of reattachment. Within seconds, the same thing happened to Brochan, searing pain ebbing and flowing.

He gritted his teeth. *Deserved.* He'd come for the goddess, not because he hoped to destroy her, as he should, but because he continued to lust after her.

Shame inundated him. Today, Brochan existed only to save his brother. Once he secured the lad in Nevaeh where time ceased to exist, McCadden would live forever *without* his wings or immortality. Then, oh *then*, Brochan would turn his attention to retribution at long last. There were so many ways to punish a goddess...

First things first. How did he obtain her key to Nevaeh? As soon as she'd announced to a crowd of males that she owned one, Brochan had changed course. Key first, vengeance second.

No matter how hard or often Brochan and another like-minded Forsaken named Farrow attacked the invisible veil that separated the timeless realm from every other, they failed to breach it.

"We *will* get that key," Midian vowed, panting through his pain.

Threat! Brochan's deepest instincts sharpened. Instincts he only managed to bury in spurts. *Protect the goddess at all costs.* Once an aggravation to be endured. Now a complicated but necessary endeavor.

All Forsaken combatted the same obsessive need to reenter Nevaeh. Himself included. Though his brother's reentry mattered far more to him than his own. Now these males would stop at nothing to obtain Viola.

"Get in our way," Midian snapped, "and we'll rally the others. We'll kill your brother outright and torture the goddess before she, too, greets death."

Brochan laughed, the sound as crazed as he sometimes—always—felt. "Go ahead. Strike at my brother and the goddess en masse." Three of the most powerful Sent Ones in existence guarded McCadden; Brochan made sure of it. As for Viola, the warriors must get through him to reach her. No one got through him. "I'll turn my sights to *you*. Nothing pleases me more than the misery of my foes. You know this better than most."

Malice pulsed from the other male. "Will I receive the same misery as the goddess? Tell me, mighty Broken. What horrors have you visited upon her, hmm?"

Brochan snared a curse, soon losing track of everything but his agony. Bones, muscles and arteries wove back together. Organs revived, and his lungs refilled. By the time he regained control of his limbs, no hint of his civility remained.

Inhalations coming shallow and fast, he jolted into an upright position—just in time to catch a swinging fist. Midian had gained control a split second before him. Maintaining an unyielding hold, Brochan came to his feet with a flap of his wings. Rather than attack, he hissed and shoved the other Forsaken.

Midian bumped into Joseph, who had just flashed into the cell. He snapped, "We *will* get the key from the goddess. One way or another."

The two vanished, and Brochan barely stifled the urge to find the goddess. To punish her...to feast his gaze upon her again. To taste her lips at long last.

Gritting his teeth, he planted his feet and rolled his newly attached head from shoulder to shoulder. Bones popped, and mended flesh stretched. He stretched his wings too, blinking when he noticed ten ivory hooks protruding from the joints. Those hooks hadn't been there before his run-in with Viola.

Well, well. This particular change earned his whole-hearted approval.

From experience, he knew three days had passed since his death. And yet, Viola's sweet perfume hadn't faded in the slightest, roses eclipsing the putrid stench of past tortures. He breathed deeply, because he must. The drugging fragrance fogged his head, kindling little fires in his blood, somehow calming and inciting him to violence all at once.

Where was she now?

Brochan had paid good money for the mystical tattoo etched into his forearm. A blood link forbidden to Sent Ones. The connection kept him apprised of Viola's emotional state and location. As she relocated, the map changed, allowing him to flash straight to her.

She had no idea he tracked her this way or that he remained aware of her emotions. No one did. It was his deepest shame. Oh, how far he had fallen. How much farther would he fall?

He studied the lines and dots staining his flesh. Ah. Currently, his goddess inhabited the mortal realm. Specifically, a place called Oklahoma. She'd visited the area before. A land where wolf packs easily blended with society.

What should Brochan do with her now that other Forsaken suspected she owned a key to Nevaeh?

He must craft a plan before their next interaction. He should also visit his brother's keepers.

Hands fisted, he flashed to the Downfall, where McCadden worked. The immortal nightclub was housed in a building with four floors, the club itself on the bottom, with offices and living quarters up above. Located in the third level of the skies, it was easily accessible by anyone with wings or an ability to flash or teleport.

Two burly bouncers—both Sent Ones—stood guard at the red double doors in front.

"I will speak with Thane, Bjorn or Xerxes." Brochan's gravelly voice turned the command into a threat.

The pair knew him by sight and no longer reacted to his less-than-stellar appearance. Though they said nothing aloud and remained in place, Xerxes arrived in the doorway soon after. All Sent Ones wielded the ability to communicate telepathically. A fellowship Brochan had lost when he fell, his connection to his fellow warriors severed. Another reason to despise Viola.

The white-haired, scarred Xerxes stood as tall as Brochan and just as strong. Eyes the color of radioactive blood gleamed with a surprising amount of concern. He wore a white robe, golden wings arching over broad shoulders. Those wings revealed his rank: an Elite 7. The fiercest and most unrelenting of soldiers.

Despite Brochan's fall from grace, he considered Xerxes an ally. "What's happened?"

"There are Forsaken determined to capture McCadden and use him against me. Be ready."

"Always." Xerxes waved him inside. Trimmed nails tipped his fingers rather than repulsive claws. One of a thousand differences between them. "Come in and speak with your brother. He's worried about you."

"I will come inside. I will not speak with McCadden." Until Brochan found a way into Nevaeh or handled Viola once and for all, he had nothing of value to offer the boy—man—he'd raised.

"Tell me why," Xerxes insisted.

"No." Brochan wasted no more time, flashing to the attic apartment he kept at the Downfall. The door remained closed and locked, no one able to witness his entrances or exits. He showered and changed into clean leathers but left his feet bare. As usual. Sharp demon claws tipped his toes, as well. The sight made his jaw clench.

After gathering an array of weapons, he returned to the barren wasteland he'd claimed as his personal territory. A world without water, foliage, or life he'd discovered a year ago. He resided in the realm's only remaining structure: a dusty, musty palace topping a steep hill. The king and queen's suite, specifically. Though Brochan conducted all business in the throne room. High ceilings allowed for easy flight.

Despite frequent visits, he'd left the palace in its abandoned state. A black cloth draped the throne. Material covered most of the portraits on the walls, as well. The visible images displayed past monarchs. Warlocks and witches. A lone skeleton leaned against the bottom of the throne as if someone had curled up in a favorite spot after doing their best to preserve the artifacts of a dead civilization.

As Brochan strode to the table he'd pushed to the center of the chamber, broken glass shards sliced his heels. The stinging injuries proved minimal, yet he left a trail of blood in his wake. Oh, well. This wasn't the first time, and it wouldn't be the last.

Books and ancient scrolls littered the tabletop, most depicting a tale about Viola. In his quest for vengeance, he'd managed to cobble together bits and pieces of her past.

The earliest known sighting? An obscure reference to a "beautiful, golden-haired goddess of the Afterlife, who fed on souls." Origins unknown, said to be cold, cruel and heartless. The next mention told of a crime committed against the goddess Dione, first wife of Zeus. Both former power players among the Greeks. Reports suggested this golden-haired beauty slaughtered Dione's servants for entertainment.

Cold and cruel, Brochan understood. But heartless? No. No one loved harder than Viola. She loved herself utterly, madly, completely. So, clearly, she had a heart. It was shriveled, yes, but it was a heart nonetheless, which meant she did have a weakness. He had only to find it.

Brochan grabbed the scroll with a sketch of Viola. A type of mugshot, he thought the humans called it. Dione had meted out revenge, arranging for Viola's incarceration in Tartarus, where she had spent centuries.

A young Viola peered up at him from the page, her expression startled, her hair wild and in tangles.

His chest clenched. He traced a fingertip across her lips and scowled. *Beautiful on the outside. Monstrous on the inside.* Selfish. Haughty. As brutal as advertised. Everything he'd once fought against in the skies. But...

She was also charming without effort. Wonderfully confident, no matter the situation. Never shy or soft-spoken, as his wives had been. No, Viola took what she wanted, when she wanted it, and let nothing stop her. A commendable trait. An *insufferable* trait. But even still, Brochan hungered for her.

Fool! Every foul thing she did, she did with one aim: to save that devil-dog. As if her bloodthirsty pet was worth more than McCadden. Or anyone.

If Brochan must watch his brother age and die, Viola must experience the same with her darling Fluffy. He expected—nay, he *demanded*—tit for tat.

Temper flaring, he fixed his attention on the story of the goddess's imprisonment. For centuries, Viola languished in her cell, locked in solitary confinement. At some point, she became bonded to Narcissism.

According to the warden's report, that bond was forced upon her. Brochan refused to feel sorry for her, however. He—

The tattoo on his arm heated, and he tossed the scroll with a huff. Viola was excited about something. On the prowl for a gullible immortal already? This could not be borne.

Fury bubbled inside him. But so did anticipation. The time for observation and hoping the goddess inadvertently revealed the key to Nevaeh ended now.

A quick plan formed. *Bring her here. Imprison her until she gifts the key. Choose her ultimate fate.* His lust for her hadn't mattered, didn't matter, and wouldn't matter.

Decided, Brochan unsheathed a blade and flashed away.

Chapter Three

Not him. His aura burned too bright.

Not him. His aura indicated a rageful temper.

Not him. His aura spoke of fear. No courage.

Music blasted as Viola strutted through a crowded nightclub packed with wolfshifters, searching the sea of faces. Three days had passed since Brochan's demise, and she'd barely thought of him more than a hundred times. Practically never when you considered that most people had trillions of thoughts a day. But...

She maybe, kinda, sorta did possibly, perhaps miss the stimulation of his insistent chase. Having such a dedicated bodyguard hadn't sucked. At least Brochan could no longer stop her from feeding Fluffy or temporarily quieting Narcissism. Exactly what she planned to do tonight.

The fur-baby required a full battery recharge, and the demon demanded adoration. Winning a man's heart provided both. For a short time, at least.

Two birds, one slightly distasteful stone. Hardly a big deal. The pangs now arching through her meant nothing.

For two days, she'd failed at her mission. But not tonight. Victory was critical. Soon, the demon would begin siphoning *her* confidence, leaving her vulnerable against the mountain of insecurities and loathing buried beneath her glorious self-assurance. A circumstance she abhorred—as anyone would. Her tears never ceased and fears constantly overran her mind.

Confidence was her drug of choice, and she planned to get smashed. So. *Here we are.* Viola endeavored to do what she hated and loved: charm someone into falling in love with her.

Exactly as she'd done to McCadden and so many others. Meaning, another family would be devastated.

Her chest tightened, squeezing her rib cage.

You deserve better, Narcissism whispered. *Always better.*

Yes. She did.

Tightening further… Why should she care about others, anyway? People might not mean to, may actively try not to or have the best intentions, but they always betrayed you. It happened without fail. But oh, how she yearned to torment the fiend the way he so often tormented her. If anyone deserved to suffer, he did. But how was she supposed to fight a monster responsible for her confidence?

Just get this done and move on.

Lights flashed as randy wolfshifters flailed and thrashed upon the dance floor. *Not him. Not him. Not him.* As usual, she sought a specific type of male. Someone eager for love but also courting death. Her gift to *herself.* Selecting males on the verge of dying kept all guilt at bay…mostly. At least half, surely. Why should she allow death to extinguish so much power? Why not remove the power first? Win-win.

Viola was born with an ability to read auras. A prized skill, to be sure. Auras shared the deepest secrets. The condition of a heart, whether pure or evil. The state of a mind, whether at peace or agitated. The amount of time someone had left, whether centuries or hours.

Now that she thought about it, Brochan and his fellow winged Fallen Ones hadn't sported an aura. Why? What did it mean?

"Hey, sexy—" someone called.

"No," she said without pause. *Not him, not him. Not—hmm. Him?* Her steps slowed as she examined the male more thoroughly.

He perched alone at the end of the bar, nursing a drink. His head hung with dejection. The soft glow of his aura revealed a tortured soul steeped in misery. Dark spots grew from the edges. Death had already sunk sharp hooks into his future.

She peered closer at him. No oily residue marred his aura, suggesting an immortal disease, yet she knew he only had two weeks. Maybe three. He was going to die. Why not gift him with the best week of his life? Seven days of stimulating conversation, laughs, and kindness before she claimed his immortality and jetted, leaving him to die as a mortal rather than an immortal. Or seven hours. Yes, she liked that timeframe better. He would too probably.

I'm practically a humanitarian. His family should thank her for her services. At the very least, they should offer her endless gifts of homage. Something Brochan should have done.

Her chest tightened again. What if things had been different? What if she hadn't killed the Fallen One? What if she'd explained how perilously close McCadden had stood at the cliff between life and death before she stepped in instead? Would he have thanked her for her actions? Not that she cared. So the tightening worsened. So what? A bout of heartburn, most likely. No big deal. Moving on.

Yes, she'd found her man. Excitement without a single hint of guilt—not even the slightest drop, honest!—fizzed in her veins. Wearing a slinky white dress with a super-short hem and a deep vee to best display her ample cleavage, she sauntered over.

She slid into the chair beside him and offered a greeting with a voice as potent as an erotic caress. "Hello, handsome."

He jolted, startled before shifting his gaze to her. Frowning, he pointed to his chest. "Me?"

"Why not you?" she asked with the world's most enchanting laugh. As much as she disliked the necessity of this, she also kind of enjoyed it. Flirting freely, earning adoration. Interacting with others. Living! Everything she'd been denied while whiling away the years in each of her prisons.

Leave the past in the past. "I'm Viola, your newest obsession. And no, you're not dreaming. I'm not some figment of your imagination." She offered him a dazzling smile and traced a fingertip across his brow, leaving a spiritual mark only she and Fluffy could sense, ensuring easy tracking if they got separated. "I'm here, and I'm real."

He peered at her, dazed—surely—allowing the touch without flinching or commenting. "I just want to be left alone, ma'am."

Ma'am. Ma'am? *He dies* today!

Think of Fluffy. Deep breath in. Out. Viola curbed her murderous urges. But he deserved what was coming now, and that was that.

She pasted an even more dazzling smile. "If someone can't charm you into changing your mind within a five-minute span, they're a slacker. I'll do it in four. Are you willing to give me a chance?"

His brow furrowed, his confusion obvious. "You wish to charm me? Why?"

She leaned closer, telling him, "Better question. Why *wouldn't* I want to?" A strange sensation prickled on her nape, and she glanced up.

Gasped. No way she saw what she thought she did. This...this...it was impossible. Wasn't it?

"I don't understand," the wolfshifter said.

"Neither do I." A trick of the light? *Please be a trick.*

The music stopped abruptly, every shifter in the spacious building halting. The once-headless Brochan stood at the back of the room, alive and well—and clearly incensed.

But, but... "I decapitated him. *Like a boss,*" she said, jumping to her feet. She wobbled on her towering stilettos. Was he a ghost, come to haunt her?

Brochan was shirtless, wearing only a pair of black leathers. Standard mythological warrior attire rather than ghostly. Although, other warriors wore boots. His feet were bare. His skin appeared a deeper shade of blue than before, his facial features sharper, and his wings larger. Her heart fluttered. Bone hooks protruded from the joints. Lethal danger radiated from him, chilling her.

Curses and threats rang out around him as her companion leaped to his feet.

"Get behind me," he commanded, moving in front of her. "I will protect you."

As if! No one protected her better than herself. A lesson she'd learned as a vulnerable child, courtesy of her mother.

As she stepped around him, the shifters roared their wrath over the unwelcome intrusion. Black shadows seeped from their pores, growing together to create a wolfish mask from head to toe.

The moisture in her mouth dried. No, no trick of light or ghost. He was here, he was real, and staring right at her.

How had Brochan recovered from *a missing head?* Not even she could do that, and she could do absolutely anything better than anyone, her talents and abilities unlimited.

The mutated Fallen One stood across the room, his gaze remaining fixed on her. A maniacal glint lit his silver irises, his grim expression bordering on homicidal. He might have shown her mercy before, but he wouldn't do so again. The promise of agony emanated from him, his muscles hardening.

"I've decided what I will do with you," he proclaimed for one and all to hear.

His deep, husky timbre roused a wealth of goose bumps. She faked a yawn. "You're planning to give me a front massage, aren't you?"

He blinked and growled. "Not a massage. But hands will be involved."

The second he stepped forward, the shifters flew into motion, pouncing on him. Brochan went high and then low, left then right, remaining in a constant state of motion as he made his way toward her. No one felled him. A few wolves clawed his arms and torso, but they didn't slow him, and they suffered greatly for their efforts. In retaliation, Brochan tore off their limbs. Like, all of them. Arms and legs. His claws were much bigger and far sharper.

Viola watched, mesmerized. In battle, he was magnificent, full stop. Fierce and unrelenting. Utterly savage. Such strength! He was determined to reach her, whatever the cost. Did he even know how sexy that was? Her heart fluttered, and her palms dampened. He remained pitiless against anyone foolish enough to approach him. Wreaking havoc, he spun, flaring and retracting his wings as necessary. His opponents dropped, groups at a time, unable to stand. Or breathe.

But even as Brochan killed, he kept his gaze on Viola's companion. When the male eased closer, the beast flared his horns and swung his claws with more force.

She inched away from the shifter, increasing the distance between them, and Brochan returned to a normal speed.

Okay. All right. Her nearness might get Fluffy's meal axed sooner rather than later.

Confidence cracking, Narcissism retaliated against *her*, releasing a kernel of fear. Vines slithered from it, one after the other, each tipped by a memory. Growing stronger. Stronger.

She had battle skill, grit and wiles, but she might not have enough skill, grit and wiles to defeat this male. But retreat? Never! Still, a timeout could help matters. A few months, years, or centuries to really think things through before she hunted him down and continued their war, soundly defeating him. Of course. Later today, once her chosen target had escaped the bar, she'd find him and reintroduce herself.

Yes. Perfect plan. No flaws, as usual. Fate must agree. The shifter's aura hadn't changed, so, he wouldn't be dying via Brochan's rage.

"Go home," she told the male. "We'll chat later. I promise." Viola flashed to a remote island in the mortal realm, leaving the shifters to deal with the beast. *My gift to you.*

Waves lapped at glistening white sands, instantly soothing her nerves. The scent of coconut and salt saturated over-warm air. Breathing deeply, she dropped into the gritty warmth, hitting her knees and—

"No!"

Brochan appeared a few yards in front of her, bathed in sunlight. But, but... How had he found her so swiftly?

Heart thudding, she rocketed to her feet and yanked off her bracelet. The same one she'd used to remove his head. With a flick of her wrist, the jewelry locked into a sword, and she squared off with him. Why, why, why didn't he have an aura? Was he death itself or something?

"How are you alive?" she demanded.

He narrowed his eyes. "Nothing has the power to kill me, goddess. Especially not you."

Oh, that cut. She could do *anything*. "I bet I'll find a way." In fact, an idea already percolated...

"You cannot escape me. Not now, not ever. No matter how many times I die, I'll always come back for you." He took a single step closer, nothing but aggression and menace. "I'll just be angrier."

Shivers of dread slipped down her spine. Definitely dread. Not excitement.

"You ensured my brother's end, and you took my life," he continued. "From this moment forward, I own yours."

She inched backward. Not because she was cowed but because she had a brain. Common sense said: *Stay away from the murdering monster.*

Her core offered multiple objections. *Get closer...*

Raising the sword, she grated, "I can strike at you in ways others cannot."

He remained unperturbed. "Strike at me all you wish. Before, you caught me off guard. This time, I'm prepared."

Not exaggeration but the unvarnished truth. Anyone who fought an entire pack of wolfshifters without breaking a sweat wielded a skill set far beyond hers. Again, she inched backward. "I won't hand over the key to Nevaeh." She couldn't. But, if he persisted in assuming she owned it, well, he would fight to keep her safe, even from himself.

Gorgeous bombshell—brilliant mastermind.

"You *will* hand it over, goddess. That, I promise you." All that gravel in his voice had taken on a guttural edge. "Until you do, you'll live in my home. If you run, I'll drag you back. If you ambush me, I'll punish you. If you disobey me, even once, I'll punish you *worse*."

Narcissism peeked from a corner of her awareness. More self-assured by the moment, the fiend prowled through the corridors of her mind.

Soon, it brimmed with possibilities. To win the heart of a beast...was there a more ultimate conquest? To crush his heart afterward... The demon grew positively giddy.

No. She would rather kill Brochan than work her wiles on him. Fluffy couldn't dine on his poisonous immortality. What's more, Viola didn't *want* to win and crush him. Which she could totally do. If she tried, even a little. He wasn't worth her time. He planned to lock her up.

A shudder racked her. Why not confess the truth? What harm could it do? "Your brother was weeks away from a true death. *Without* my aid, thank you. When I took his immortality, I altered his fate and actually prolonged his life. I did you both a favor. So. I'll hear your thanks now."

"You'll hear my thanks. Now." Flash. He appeared directly in front of her, glaring as he clamped a big, callused hand against her throat. The tips of his claws rested against her skin, and her pulse jumped. He held her weapon at bay with his other hand.

Of course, he'd doubted her. Why wouldn't he? They were foes of circumstance. The very reason she hadn't tried to explain her motives before this.

"You would say anything to save yourself," he growled.

"Yes ," she admitted, and he blinked as if startled. "But truth remains truth, regardless of your acceptance or rejection."

"How convenient for you, then, that this particular truth can't be proven." He tightened his grip on her. "McCadden loved you, and you betrayed him."

Had the Sent One truly loved her? Maybe. Had he tempted her to spare him, to fight side by side and change his fate another way? Definitely. Every male she'd ever charmed had tempted her to show mercy. Viola might be a wee bit self-involved, but she had a lot of love to give. Just ask Fluffy. So, always before she siphoned someone's immortality, she offered a loyalty test. A lone question with a single correct response. Throughout the years, she'd heard only wrong answers.

"Countless individuals have loved me," she said, lifting her chin. "Should I cater to them all?"

Brochan caressed his thumb along the side of her throat, leaving a trail of warmth. That heat spread, drawing shivers. "Do you feel a shred of remorse, goddess? I bet you'd harm my brother a second time if given the chance."

No need to ponder her reply. "You'd win that bet." To save Fluffy, she would do anything to anyone at any time.

Again, Brochan blinked, her honesty a surprise. He squeezed her throat, just enough to constrict her airways, and hissed, "Perhaps I should give you to my comrades. They're coming for you, and they crave your blood as much as the key. Perhaps more so."

The others had resurrected too? How could that be?

Desperate to process the information, Viola braced to flash, the perfect destination in mind. A land for those on the run. He'd never be able to find her. Then the ramifications of his words registered, and she planted her feet, staying put. Maybe she didn't need to evade Brochan, after all. Perhaps she should stay with him, using him as a shield against the other winged Fallen Ones.

She would *let* him imprison her until she decided to ditch him again.

A mother must sometimes suffer for the health and wellbeing of her child.

"Fine," she said with an exaggerated sigh. "I'm convinced. I'll go with you. But only because I'm so generous. Just know I expect unparalleled living quarters. Pure luxury. Also, I get to feed my baby without any more interference from you." Too tired to follow as usual, Fluffy awaited her at their current hideaway. "The nonsense stops now."

His gaze all but spit fire. "Be thankful I allow your pet to take its next breath, goddess."

She bristled. "How dare you? He is my *child*. And my terms are nonnegotiable, beast."

"And yet you're coming with me, never to see your devil-dog again." He squeezed her wrist until she mewled in pain and dropped the blade. Not because she had to. She didn't—for real, she didn't. She could hold on forever if she wanted. Keyword: *if*.

She would rather mount a proper defense. Except, he wound both of her arms behind her back before she moved an inch, trapping her body against his.

She gasped as her breasts smashed into his chest, her nipples rubbing her dress with every ragged breath. Heart flying at warp speed, she captured his gaze. In unison, they stilled. He breathed heavier. She breathed faster. Long black lashes framed those stormy irises. An array of freckles dotted his nose.

How adorable was that?

Adorable? The man threatening to pass her to others for torture? She sneered. "Release me, Brochan. Immediately! I've changed my mind again. You aren't worthy of my company."

He flinched but jutted his chin. "You'll hear *my* terms now. The only terms that matter."

"Hardly. This is the moment we part ways." Viola flashed and— nothing. She remained in place. What the—*what?* Her brows drew together as she floundered for an explanation. Why couldn't she flash?

She struggled against him to no avail, satisfaction radiating from the beast. When she brushed against something hard—she gasped again. Whoa! Brochan liked her movements. Like, a lot. He might deny it, but he wanted her. Greatly. Her knees shook.

Perhaps she had a few loose wires in her head. For some reason, her captor had just gotten more interesting and better-looking, and she wasn't sorry.

A scowl darkened his expression, and for a moment, only a moment, she thought he might be the most beautiful male in the history of histories. Then he drew her arms forward, revealing a thin, lightweight link of metal around her left wrist. "For the rest of your days, you will obey my every command. Until I hold the key to Nevaeh in my hands, I vow you won't enjoy *any* of those days. I'll ensure you regret what you did to my brother. Perhaps I'll make you regret your birth as well."

Did he think to intimidate her? Well, mission accomplished. True imprisonment was her worst nightmare come to life. Even still, she held her ground. "How cute. The rampaging brute thinks he won a great war. Let's lower your zipper and measure your body's disagreement."

His ferocity ramped up. His lips pulled back from straight, white teeth, revealing a pair of fangs. "I would rather die for good than allow you to touch that part of me."

"A true death can be arranged." She hadn't forgotten her idea...

Fury emanated from Narcissism. The fiend prowled through her mind, stirring pots of self-hatred, punishing her for failure, just as she'd feared.

Too weak to escape this Fallen One... despised and rightfully so...only deserving of suffering and tragedy...Fluffy deserves a better mother...

What if her fur-baby died during her absence, alone and frightened, as Viola had once been? What if—No! No, no, no. Absolutely not. Viola wasn't weak. She was strong sometimes. Super strong! Why, her roundhouse kick once propelled *Chuck Norris* into yesterday.

She protected herself and her baby, whatever the cost. And if Fluffy worried or required aid, he would flash to her side. He carried a literal piece of her heart, after all, which granted him the ability. That shred of heart had been woven into his and now acted as a battery she charged with other people's immortality.

As for the Fallen One, she could manage him. She must. She had wiles Brochan had never seen, and the male *did* harbor a secret desire for her, just as she'd suspected. *The way his feverish gaze watches me even now.* As if she were already stripped and waiting in his bed…

Her confidence grew. *Oh, yeah. I've got this.* She would use him for protection and force him to admit his insatiable hunger for her. He had threatened her family—now he must suffer. Once she'd brought him to his knees, Narcissism could gorge on his admiration with Viola's compliments.

He won't walk away from me. He'll crawl.

Never again would he challenge a powerful goddess of the Afterlife.

She smiled her most wicked smile, purring, "Go ahead and mark this day in your calendar, beast. It's the day you invited your downfall." Not brag about her endgame? Hardly.

He jerked against her, his muscles knotting. "You hope to seduce me?"

"It's not as hard as that measuring stick," she said, all innocence. "Admit it. You *ache* for me."

"Whatever you do," he grated, ignoring her rasping words, "you. Will. Fail."

Viola failed at nothing. She lifted her attention to his eyes and grinned. "You're mine, beast. And soon I'll prove it."

Chapter Four

No, goddess. You are mine.

Brochan silenced a roar of trepidation…and triumph. He had secured Viola. She remained in his keeping, and there was no force great enough to take her from him. Not now, not ever. He had suffered at her hand, followed her for months. Lusted after her. Despised and captured her. Now, he owned her.

Vibrating with aggression, he flashed her to his fortress in the abandoned realm. As soon as the palace's master *suite* materialized, he severed contact and stepped back. To his consternation, he was hard as steel, his palms tingling as if desperate to bask in the softness of her skin once again.

The danger she presented…

Viola was far worse than the demon she carried. She was temptation itself. Everything Brochan had ever wanted, tucked inside the most exquisite package.

"What is this place?" she asked, her just-roused-from-bed voice eliciting visions of tangled sheets and writhing bodies. She spun, eyeing his meager belongings. "Besides a hovel, I mean."

His hands curled into fists. The elaborate pieces once housed in this chamber had reminded him of Viola. Lovely and far better than he deserved. He'd destroyed the furniture in here during his first stay, replacing it with a plain bed, a table and a chair. The only room he'd truly altered.

"Welcome to your new home, goddess. Pure luxury," he mocked. As a Sent One, he'd been unable to lie in any capacity. As a Forsaken, he had no such troubles.

The only light streamed through a cracked window flanked by ragged drapes. Dust motes twirled about, coating the walls, every piece of furniture, and even the floor. She walked here and there, pinching the grubby clothes slung over the dresser and grimacing.

"To win my heart, other males have offered vast treasures," she said. "This is an…interesting opener."

"I don't want your heart, and I offer nothing but your continued survival. *That* occurs only if you behave." Her disdain for the palace irked him. As if he couldn't provide the best for her. Better than any other. "If you don't like the condition of the room, clean it."

"Of course, of course. I'll begin cleaning right away. Just as soon as you summon the servants I'll be ordering to clean it for me."

With great delight, he informed her, "From now on, you'll be your own servant." Her other males had catered to her whims, McCadden among them. Something Brochan wasn't inclined to do. Why should he? She would never attempt to charm him, never treat him as sweetly as she'd treated the others or look at him with glittering eyes and smiling lips and mean it… No, nothing but a fantasy. She hadn't even wanted him when he'd looked his best.

"Too many have coddled and spoiled you throughout the centuries," he snapped. "Their mistake. I will not be so foolish."

Why would he crave what she'd given the others, anyway? What use had he for soft, stolen glances? Graceful brushes of her fingers against his cheek or his arm? Her body leaning *into* his?

Rather than shrinking from his obvious annoyance, she dazzled him with another false smile. "Ohhhh. I understand what's going on here. You have a French maid fetish."

"I have no fetish," he snapped. Merely thinking of this sensual female dressed in a barely-there black dress threatened to unman him. *I might have a fetish.*

Another unacceptable outcome. No one should throb for a pretty face and lush curves. Even if the owner of both had been crafted from his deepest, wildest, most secret dreams. For him. He should care about her actions—and the fruit thereof—more than anything.

"Well, lucky for you," she continued blithely, "I'm happy to play this role. Hopefully, our vigorous lovemaking will improve your mood."

Lovemaking? *Vigorous?* Sweat beaded his brow. He could count on two hands the number of sexual experiences he'd had with Samantha and

Rebecca, his only lovers. He'd rather forget the tame, uncomfortable encounters.

Am I hurting you?

No, it's fine.

Are you sure? You appear pained.

I'm sure but…are you almost done? I don't mind if you wish to hurry.

After a third unsatisfying interlude with each, he'd ceased making advances. Now, Viola baited him. Yet he wondered… Would Viola demand satisfaction?

"You'd best be careful, goddess." Narrowing his eyes and lowering his chin, he intensified his scrutiny of her. "What will you do if ever I take you up on your offer?"

"Brag," she quipped, all seduction and indulgence as she twirled a lock of pale hair.

Kindling for him. How he burned.

Close the distance. Force her to back down.

Would she back down, though? Or let him do things he'd only dared imagine during the darkest of nights?

Temptation itself…

"Why do you call me Forsaken?" she asked. "Have we already reached the cute endearment stage of our association?"

"I merely offer you a warning. You made me a Forsaken. Therefore, I will make you one."

"Got it. You speak of a species. Something I should have known. You know what that means? You guys suck at PR." Pensive, she turned to inspect more of the room. "To be clear, the Forsaken are Fallen Ones with wings, yes?"

He gave a clipped nod in response.

"Makes sense, I suppose. You are indeed forsaken, even by death. If someone removes your wings, will you become a Fallen One, mortal and killable?"

How quickly her mind worked. He shook his head. "The damage is already done. Though I welcome any attempts to remove my wings." Actually, he welcomed any excuse that allowed her to touch his body…

"Thank you for the permission, darling. I *never* would've tried to take your wings otherwise, honest. Well, almost honest." She winked at him. "Where's the bathroom?"

He popped his jaw before pointing. As if she hadn't noticed the door already.

"Wonderful. After our little skirmish on the beach, I'm positively filthy." She paused to run her gaze over the length of him as if she'd spied a tasty dessert. "I'll clean up...so we can get dirty again."

The scent of roses wafted from her as she strolled past him, sharpening his hunger. Must the temptress roll her hips like that?

When Brochan remained in place, she halted in the doorway to glance over her shoulder. A half-smile bloomed. Umber irises glittered. "You can watch me if you want."

Watch the little beauty...bathe? He swiped a hand over his gaping mouth. He'd never watched a female bathe, and he thought he might kill to do so now.

Need to see her.

Need to see her wet.

"There's no water in this realm." A reality he suddenly lamented.

"Then why do I sense it?"

She was able to sense water? A fact he hadn't known. "You are always right? Never wrong?" he asked, curious.

A tinkling laugh with the slightest edge escaped her, teasing his ears. "Hardly. I was mistaken once. The time I thought I was mistaken." She disappeared inside the confines of the bathroom. Only seconds later, she squealed with delight. "Oh, look. I was right again, as expected. We have an endless spout."

Heat lanced his spine. What other things delighted her?

Inner shake. Endless spouts were a myth. Weren't they?

He strode into the ensuite, propelled by a force greater than himself, only to jerk to a halt. The goddess stood in a spacious shower stall, a vision in her slinky white gown. The hem raised as she reached overhead to toy with the nozzle.

"Once activated, it should work with simple voice commands." As she pressed symbols around the base of the spout, clear water came bursting out, soaking her. She erupted into peals of laughter, another tinkling melody he found charming and irritating in equal measure.

Still grinning, she pivoted to confront him. So beautiful, his chest ached. So sexy, his shaft threatened to rampage past his zipper.

The fabric of her dress became transparent when wet. The sight of her robbed him of breath.

"Oops," she said, batting her lashes at him. "You seem to have a little drool at the side of your mouth."

Did he? Hunger gnawing at him, he reached up to pat his mouth without looking away from her. Dry. "You lied about something so trivial?" He slitted his eyes. Whoever lied about small things lied about all things. How many other untruths had she told him?

"I most certainly did not lie. You have *metaphorical* drool on your face. It's not my fault you don't know the difference. By the way, I'm glad you decided to watch." She traced her fingertips to her lips. "Are you ready for the show of a lifetime?"

By some miracle, he managed to lift his gaze to hers. She wouldn't really do it. His heart thudded. Would she?

Challenge sizzled between them. With slow, languid movements, she unfastened her shoulder straps. The waterlogged top swooshed down, hanging from her midriff, where cinched material held the skirt in place.

She would.

His legs shook. She wore no bra, her lush curves on exquisite display. A butterfly tattoo glittered on her torso, its wings stretching from her shoulders to the waist of her dress, where the image disappeared.

The things he longed to do to this female...

No! He had worked hard on his core of iron, ensuring his resolve remained forever unshakable. Over the centuries, myriad demons had tortured him, but none had broken him. The goddess wouldn't succeed where so many others had failed.

Derive pleasure from the one he despised? No. "Your game will fail. I'll never crave you the way McCadden did. You'll never direct me."

"Say that again when I'm fully naked." She reached behind her, loosening the skirt. A skirt she held in place. "Neither of us will believe you, but we'll get to laugh about it later."

Brochan went motionless, his every muscle knotting. She wouldn't take this interlude further, wouldn't drop the material and bare her body to the beast who'd imprisoned her in a wasteland.

But she did. The dress smacked on the stall floor. Suddenly, Viola stood before him clad in only a pair of black high heels and a sleepy, come-hither smile.

He...she... Different urges surfaced, each more frenzied than the last. He frothed at the mouth to strip and join her. To press her against the tile and...do things. To hear her cry his name again and again and again.

Treacherous seductress.

Resist!

"You were saying?" she prompted, winding a lock of hair around her finger. "Something about my game failing."

He grated, "I won't bed you or pardon you for the crimes you committed against my brother. You ruined a precious life for the sake of your pride and a devil-dog." A reminder for her as much as himself.

"Yes, I did," she said, surprising him with her honesty once again. She ducked under the spray, droplets sluicing from head to toe, momentarily mesmerizing him. "But you have no right to judge. You do the same, and you can't deny it. You'll cross any line to aid your loved one."

He *couldn't* deny it.

"Besides." She ran her fingers through her wet hair. "Everyone says I'm incredibly brave for my actions."

Look away. Just look away. A command from his fraying control. A command he did not heed. He tilted his chin instead, eyeing her through his lashes. "Are you *everyone* in this scenario?" Steam began enveloping her, reality morphing into every fantasy he'd never allowed himself to entertain—for more than a few minutes at a time. "I think you're everyone," he croaked.

"I'm certainly *your* everyone." Her lips lifted in another smile, sleepy yet sharp at the edges. "Be a dear and fetch me the essentials. Soap. Shampoo. Conditioner. A negligee. Make sure to get the best of everything. I deserve nothing less. Well?" she prompted when he remained in place. "The longer I'm forced to wait, the longer I stay in the shower."

Growling, he flashed to his room at the Downfall and hurriedly gathered an array of items from his bathroom. With a huff, he returned to Viola and dropped the bundle inside the stall.

Another squeal of delight left her as she looked everything over. "Thank you, thank you, thank you." Then she frowned and pouted. "What about my negligee? I specifically remember requesting one because your leathers got noticeably tighter the second I did."

He pursed his lips. The gratitude surprised him and perhaps even softened him. The taunting prodded his nerve endings. "You may consider the toiletries a token of my goodwill only as long as you answer my queries."

"Sure. Ask away. I have nothing to hide." She pumped shampoo into her palm. "I'm happy to discuss the world's favorite topic—me."

How could she act so natural while naked with a fully clothed male? *Not charmed by her confidence. More and more annoyed.* Her boldness kept him off-kilter. "Who are your parents?"

"Yikes. You dove straight into the deep end, huh?" She lathered her hair, every move a sensual dance. "How about this? I'll tell you their identities when you earn my trust or provide a candlelit dinner for two. Whichever comes first. Which isn't a refusal to answer, so no storming over to spank me. Not as punishment, anyway…"

He gnashed his teeth. The things she said to him! "Why keep the identity of your parents a secret?" And it was a secret. Most of the records he'd found were noticeably doctored. "Are you ashamed of your sires?"

She rinsed off and sighed. "Perhaps I am. My married mother slept with a husband, but he wasn't hers. I was the result. To conceal her actions, she hid me for over two decades. Her disloyalty to those she was supposed to love and cherish disgusts me to this day."

"In this, we are agreed. There is no viler trait than disloyalty." *Disregard the ache in your chest.* "Is she living or dead?"

Viola flinched ever so slightly. "She is dead."

I don't care if the past upsets her. This doesn't matter. Nothing changed her crimes against his family. "She disgusted you, but still you loved her." A statement, not a question.

"Well, surprise, surprise. You just ensured I *don't* like talking about myself," she muttered. As she massaged conditioner into those glorious tresses, arching her spine and thrusting up her breasts, she wrenched a sharper growl from deep in his chest. "When you requested conversation, I thought you planned to ask me about my turn-ons."

He jerked and tried to hide the action with a cough. What *did* turn her on? "Tell me where you've secreted the key, and we don't have to talk of anything at all."

In lieu of a response, she smeared soap over her torso, taking extra care in select places, daring him to try and stop her. Or comment. The scent of roses blended with the fragrance of sandalwood. Her perfume melded with his, becoming theirs.

He wiped a hand over his face. "How many immortals have you bespelled and abandoned?" A topic sure to douse the fire spreading through his veins.

"Hundreds," she replied with a breezy tone. She canted her head, thoughtful. "Times three."

"Did you bathe for any of them?" The query shoved its way through his clenched teeth.

"They wished! They never passed my test, so they never made it past first base. They weren't worthy."

McCadden hadn't bedded the goddess? Why did every cell in Brochan's body suddenly heat? "There's no greater male than my brother. He is worthy of anyone. More than worthy."

"If that's true, why did he—?" She pressed her lips together, going quiet. "I bestowed a single kiss upon him. Prize enough for his sacrifice."

He scoffed. "My brother gave up his immortality for a lone meeting of lips?"

"I'm *that* good." She rinsed her hair.

A soap bubble sluiced over peaks and planes, catching his attention, and he swallowed a groan. How he remained in place without flashing to her, he might never know. "Tell me about your test."

She moved to the bench and eased down, every inch the Victorian lady clad in ruffles and lace. Water sprayed over her outstretched legs. "I'd rather hear about you. What kind of male are you? I mean, I know you were a decorated demon assassin in the sky realms and a major irritation in whatever world we currently occupy, but little else."

She'd investigated his past? *Pretend your chest isn't puffing up.* "I was a decorated assassin, yes. I liked my job. I love my brother more."

"You fell from the skies to remain with McCadden? Wow. You value loyalty as much as I do," she said, sounding dazed. "Color me curious. Are *you* worthy of all this?" She twirled a fingertip around her navel, and he swallowed. "Let's find out. Once you've fallen in love with me, I'll give my test to you."

The sight of this woman... *Concentrate.* "What does the female who condemns innocent immortals to demise consider worthy, exactly, if not forcing a man to sign his own death warrant?"

"Trust me," she purred, "you'll find out soon."

Do not close the distance and put your hands on her.

Do not.

Do...

No! He was panting, every breath as sharp as a razor. "Finish your shower." A towel. She needed one. Yes. He flashed to the Downfall and back, terrycloth in hand. She hadn't changed positions. "You've used enough water for today."

"Sir, yes, sir." Soaked, flushed and utterly wicked, she leaned against the wall and lifted a leg into the spray. "Except... Permission to linger a bit more, sir. My thoughts are only getting dirtier. They could use a good scrubbing."

"Do not try my patience, goddess. I've treated you kindly so far." Far kinder than she deserved, going against his basest instincts. "That can change at any moment."

"What am I supposed to wear? Someone forgot to fetch me that negligee. Or am I supposed to walk around naked?"

Growling again, he returned to his room at the Downfall, where he gathered a handful of garments from his closet. He returned to the same spot and—stopped breathing. In anticipation of his arrival, Viola had switched locations. Now, she stood only a whisper away. So close he detected the golden flecks in her whiskey eyes.

His heart thudded. "Goddess?"

"I have a question for *you*," she intoned, peering up at him. Her cherry-red lips were parted, a moan of delight seeming poised for release. "How badly do you want me, beast?"

Chapter Five

Caught up in her own game? Check. Viola kept forgetting Brochan bore a terrible grudge against her. But maybe he kept forgetting too? The longer she'd showered and chatted with him, doing her best to feign nonchalance, the more intently he'd surveyed her. He struck her as a man at the end of a year-long fast, who'd just discovered the last morsel of food in existence. How could she not crave more of *that*?

She wasn't the only one. Narcissism loved every second. With each longing glance, Brochan flooded her with satisfaction and incomparable power. Was there anything better?

Why had she ever run from Brochan, anyway? Here, now, as the Forsaken radiated great waves of heat, she wished to sidle closer to him. For her mission, of course. Only her mission.

Will enjoy entrancing this volatile male, then punishing him for daring to threaten Fluffy.

Unless Viola did, in fact, make him fall in love with her. Should she? Added bonus: She would be punishing him so much *worse*. Lust burned brightly for but a moment. Love lasted forever.

Change a man's endgame, and you forever altered the course of his life. The moment she won Brochan's heart, his vendetta reached its end. Love conquered all, and that was an inescapable truth. She'd seen it time and time again. The moment the Forsaken loved her, he would long only to protect and pleasure her. Harm Fluffy? Never again. He might even offer Viola the same loyalty he granted McCadden.

Loyalty was her kryptonite, and Brochan's exhibition of it was oh, so enticing.

As amazing and wonderful and perfect and glorious and magnificent and exquisite and brilliant and delightful as she was, she *deserved* such loyalty. Yet, no suitor had ever demonstrated devotion equal to hers.

Before Viola accepted a gift of immortality from a male, she presented him with the opportunity of a lifetime: *Betray <insert the name of his most cherished loved one>, and I'll stay with you forever.* No one had ever responded correctly.

Brochan dropped the bundle of clothing at her feet. Even as he heaved his breaths while repeatedly fisting and opening his hands, he reminded her of a statue. Cold. Hard. Intractable. "Remove yourself from me, goddess." The hoarse command lacked substance.

"Happy to," she told him with a silky undertone. She brushed the tip of her nose against his. "After you answer my question." In case he'd forgotten it, she said, "How badly do you want me? If you'd rather not get into the nitty-gritty details, a simple *more than anything* will do."

"Understand me now. I will *never* take you," he vowed, his gaze like flint on hers. Except, his pupils were expanding, overtaking those pale irises.

He wants me bad. Who could blame him? She was naked, damp…and hungry.

"Now, now, Brochan. That isn't an acceptable answer. It's a lie." She wound her arms around his shoulders and toyed with the ends of his dark hair. "Besides, think back. I never offered you the use of my body. I merely inquired about your overwhelming feelings on the matter."

His eyelids drooped, his calm mask slipping. Just enough to offer a glimpse of the uncivilized beast lurking beneath the surface. "Feelings have no bearing on the situation," he grated. "Overwhelming or otherwise."

Adorable monster, with his long, curling lashes and freckles. Aggressive warrior, with his harsh features and big body, simmering hotter and hotter. *Sexy* body. The most muscular one in existence—a visual feast! Faultless.

How had he not exploded already? Better question: How far did she want this to go?

Voice low and silky, she asked, "No bearing on the situation? Not ever? Because I'm feeling a need to be kissed by you. Surely you've wondered how good I taste…"

A growl rumbled in his chest. "I owe you nothing, goddess. Not answers. Certainly not a kiss." He settled his grip on her hips, lifted her, and set her a few feet away from him. Seconds passed, but he maintained his hold, never releasing her. He began to pant. "I should let the other Forsaken have you."

"Do they put out? Because I might go willingly." As she awaited his next move, cool air lapped at heated flesh. What would he do? "I'd do anyone right now. Obviously."

He narrowed his eyes and tightened his clasp, squeezing before lifting her a second time and placing her directly in front of him. "You should curry my favor."

"Or you should curry mine. I'm quite handsy when I'm happy. By the way, I'm happiest when I'm safe…and recovering from an orgasm."

His gaze slid to her lips, and he gulped.

Oh, yes. He wants me. Awareness of him seared her brain, her every cell. Sizzling arousal rushed through her veins. Her limbs trembled. She should have undressed and showered for this male sooner.

In a day, perhaps two, Brochan would be so besotted, he'd do anything she asked, even acquire an energy boost for Fluffy. Then, they could work together to ensure the forever murder of the Forsaken.

Everything was falling into place quite nicely.

"I like this half-maiden, half-conqueror thing you've got going on," she told him, dragging her blunt-tipped nails along his scalp. "Yeah, you're right. You probably shouldn't kiss me. I'd be super into it." When she brushed the base of a horn, his breath hitched. A delightful reaction. "And you do hope to punish me, yes?"

"Hope? No. I will." Moving too swiftly to track, he gripped her throat. A favorite hold, apparently. As he angled her chin higher, his claws pricked the length of her carotid. Why, why, why did the action thrill her? "Understand me, goddess. I'm not one of your conquests. I'll *never* be one of your conquests."

Are you sure, beast? "Very well. If you don't want to bend me over that bench and slam into me from behind, that is your prerogative. Let's hammer out the details of our partnership instead." With every word she uttered, her throat moved against his palm, a shockingly erotic caress. "With my help, you can destroy the other Forsaken."

"Choose my brother's treacherous ex over my own kind?" He glared down at her, a man at war, the battlefield harsh and bloody. "Why would I ever?"

"For starters, I look better naked."

"You…do," he grated, grinding his erection between her legs.

Tendons pulled taut as if he fought his actions. Fought and failed.

A gasp of delight escaped her. "Also, they are your competition. They, too, seek the key. Do you honestly believe they'll share it with you, if they get it?" She pushed her advantage. "Plus, you crave me."

"You speak of pleasure." Narrowed eyes, strained tone. He grazed the pad of his thumb over her racing pulse point. "I thought we killed that line of conversation."

"We did. But you brought it back to life with groin-to-groin resuscitation."

His mask of civility slipped again. Holding her gaze, he moved his big, callused hands to her sides—his *trembling* hands. Her breath caught with the realization. He was a steady warrior...until she neared.

Trembling just as forcefully, she awaited his next move. One minute passed. Two. They stood still and silent, staring at each other.

"What are you waiting for, Brochan?" The neediness in her voice embarrassed her because it wasn't feigned. She continued anyway. "Taste me already. I want your lips on mine."

He shook his head, but the war inside him visibly intensified, his breaths coming faster. Strain seemed to coil in his every muscle. Then...

"This means nothing." With a growl, he swooped down and slammed his mouth over hers. He wasn't shy or tentative about kissing her, but he wasn't finessed, either. He used force, thrusting his tongue against hers, conquering with abandon, taking everything and demanding more.

Viola kissed him back with equal fervor but far more gently. While his passion fueled her internal fires, she had no desire to speed to the finish line. She was a fine wine. She should be sampled slowly and savored.

Soon, he responded to the gentler laps. He licked and sucked and moaned, his appetite for her unrivaled. She clung to him, desperate for more and more and more.

As he glided those big, rough hands along her back, grazing his claws against the ridges of her spine, she shivered. Then he cupped her backside, yanking her closer and erasing the final gap of air between them. Suddenly, her every heaving inhalation sparked an agonizing friction.

"More," she demanded.

An error on her part. The split-second pause allowed his fury to rear its ugly head. With a roar, he wrenched his mouth from hers.

Remaining in place, panting, he glared at her, still clasping her tight.

Tighter. "I was right. It meant absolutely nothing!"

"Let's make it mean even less." Nonplussed, she rose to her tiptoes, gripped one of his horns and—argh!

He jumped backward, dislodging her grip. Though fuming, he didn't flash off. Or use the separation to calm. No, appearing wilder by the second, he backed her into the wall, walking through steam and hot water without concern for his leathers. His attention remained laser-focused on her as he braced his palms beside her temples.

Voice nothing but smoke and gravel, he said, "You shouldn't have touched my horn, goddess."

"Why? Did I summon your basest instincts?"

"Yes," he hissed, pressing her against cool stone. "Why must you be so beautiful?" Despite his harsh tone, he kneaded her hip, winning a new gasp from her. As she melted into his touch, his eyes blazed. "Why must you look, smell and *feel* like paradise?"

"The answer strikes me as obvious. I *am* paradise, Brochan."

"That's not—never mind." He nipped her bottom lip. "Tell me if I do something you do not enjoy."

So far, she had no complaints. "You won't know by my reactions?" Something warm and sweet spread through her. She tilted her head to the side. "Are you a virgin, Brochan?" Many Sent Ones were.

Cheeks reddening, he made to turn away from her. She sank her sharp pink claws into his shoulders. And yes, he was strong enough to break her hold. But he didn't.

"Well?" she prompted, continuing to use that soft, smooth tone. He remained rooted in place, his rich, woodsy scent filling her nose. "Are you?"

"I am not," he snapped, defensive to the max.

"But…?"

"But." He glared down at her as if she were to blame for whatever information was poised for escape. "I had not experienced a kiss before. Both females offered me their cheeks."

The sweet, warmth coated every inch of Viola, parts of her tingling with anticipation. "Foolish girls. I enjoyed your kiss very much. In fact, I demand another right this second." She clasped his nape and rose to her tiptoes, claiming his mouth with hers.

He did nothing to stop her. Rather, he encouraged her, his shockingly soft lips inviting her deeper. That softness…especially compared to the hardness of the rest of him… She quaked against his strength.

Their tongues rolled together, both giving and taking. Then he took the reins of control, kissing her the same way he fought. Fierce and wild. Primal and real. Raw. He feasted on her mouth, holding nothing back.

She melted into him, fusing their bodies, and he rocked against her. Arcs of pleasure left her gasping. Her heart thudded, igniting an erratic pulse in different parts of her. Aches ebbed and flowed, soon trapping her in a never-ending cycle of anticipation and desperation.

"There is *nothing* better than this." He hooked an arm beneath one of her knees, unleashing his inner caveman. "Never want to stop."

Good. Better than good. "Never stop," she echoed.

Rocking... "Never held anything as perfect as you."

His praise went straight to her head. Growing drunk on him, Viola scraped her nails along the root of his wings. Shivers rippled through the silken, ebony tissue, so she did it again.

Moaning, he moved the flanks of those magnificent wings to her sides, blocking out the rest of the world. She grazed a fingertip over a dangerous joint hook, delighting at his newest shiver. Lifting her arms, she grazed his torso, his scalp...his horns.

Those horns stood straighter, all *thank you very much*. Had any male ever responded so fervently or quickly to her?

He rocked with more force.

A whimper escaped, her need for him amplifying. He adored her. Obviously. The kind of adoration she'd always deserved. If he continued this, she would blossom like a rose, empowered for weeks, months. Years! Outside of the bedroom, he would do everything in his considerable power to make her happy. Surely! And, and, and...she didn't care about anything else right now. She only desired more of Brochan.

Narcissism whirred and purred, ravenous to control a male as powerful as the Forsaken—a chance to win him, to hurt him and cause untold pain.

Getting too caught up. Red alert! This isn't a drill. Viola did what she had to do to help Fluffy and save herself. And yes, she absolutely positively planned to use then lose Brochan for his threats against her family. Maybe. Probably. The thing she wouldn't do? Cater to a horrid demon's personal amusement.

She should end this kiss now, before things went too far. She should—

Brochan gave a guttural shout and disengaged from her mouth, inch by inch. First, he lifted his head. Then he peeled his chest from hers...his lower body, and released her leg, allowing her to stand on her own power. *Then* he stepped back, ensuring no part of them touched. A chill rushed over her.

Reeling, Viola fought for breath. She couldn't make sense of what had just happened. He had stopped the kiss? *He* had? He'd *dared*? But why?

Was it possible...? No, it couldn't be. Except, what if his will *was* stronger than hers?

But, but... She preferred to win, not lose. Didn't he realize that?

A new whimper attempted to escape, but she clenched her teeth. The war wasn't lost. She could change Brochan's mind. Could make him see things her way.

"You told me to bring anything I don't like to your attention," she said as casually as she could manage. "Well, you did something I didn't like. You stopped."

He sucked in a breath. Then he flashed outside the stall and picked up the towel he'd dropped. Averting his gaze, he offered the linen to her. "Turn off the water. Dry and get dressed. You have clothing and no excuses now."

The war might be lost.

Though her knees trembled, she jutted her chin and strutted over, accepting the gift. As she dressed, he pivoted, offering his back.

Her movements turned jerky. "Are you going to tell me *why* you stopped?" Excellent. She sounded curious rather than hurt. Because she wasn't hurt. She'd have to care for him to experience hurt over a rejection, and she didn't care. Not even a little. "Did you recall the fact that someone with such a hideous face isn't good enough for me?"

Hurt me, and I hurt you worse. But again, she wasn't hurt. And she still didn't care.

Stiff as a board, he told her, "You'll find nourishment in the throne room. As long as you remain in the fortress, you'll be safe. No need to worry that you'll be harmed. There are no threats here, because you are the only resident. I'll return in a week or so—"

What! "Did you say a week? Or so? You're *leaving*?" He planned to abandon her? "And what do you mean, the only resident?" To while away her days without companionship, exactly as she'd done as a child in her mother's forgotten palace? At least in Tartarus, there'd been living beings in the cell next to hers. "I require an adoring public!" she shrieked, panic budding.

"And yet you won't get one."

The panic mutated into full-blown hysteria. "Don't leave me here, Brochan. Please!" Was she begging? Yes! Her pride was nowhere to be found. "I promise I'll be good. I won't kiss you again, honest. I won't even shower. Okay? Just stay here and—"

"Goodbye, goddess." Not giving her time to formulate a different reply, he flashed, disappearing, leaving her alone with her fears.

* * * *

She is my brother's killer.

My obsession.

No matter the protest, Brochan failed to kick the goddess out of his head. Livid, he materialized in his bedroom at the Downfall. He stalked into his closet and exchanged soaked leathers for dry.

The way Viola had kissed him…. *I'm that good*, she'd said. Yes. Yes, she was. Still he hungered for her, the intensity of his desires nearly overshadowing his concerns and defenses.

If only he hadn't felt her emotions. Her excitement. Her pleasure. Her *dis*pleasure. She'd stiffened in his arms before getting lost in her thoughts. What had he done that she hadn't liked? Or had Viola only pretended with him? What if she'd imagined someone else at first?

He bit his tongue. She'd only sought to manipulate Brochan. Exactly as she'd manipulated so many others before him. Kiss—addict him—then demand he provide her with the world for the promise of another taste.

Temptation itself…

But he knew better. He did!

Someone must have heard him stomping around because a knock sounded at the door. "Brother? You have returned?"

McCadden.

Tension stole through him with record speed, betrayal fast on its heels. Speak to his brother, mere seconds after kissing the woman McCadden once loved? How could he dare?

Like a coward, Brochan flashed to the very edge of Nevaeh—to the veil between it and the rest of the skies. He glided his wings, hovering in the night sky. Despite the location change, he couldn't escape Viola's panic. He felt it as surely as he'd felt everything else. A trick. Only a trick. She didn't like the idea of being denied her pet or adoration, that was all. And yet, unease crept over him.

Focus. The wants and desires of his foe meant nothing.

The veil stretched before him, invisible and indestructible. Beyond it, a terrain of dewy flowers carpeted hill after hill. A land untouched by evil. A realm he'd once called home. Mere months ago, legions of Sent Ones had traversed this area at all hours of the day and night. Now, the spot remained abandoned, thousands of soldiers currently waging war in the Underworld.

Open season.

Another Forsaken hovered nearby. Someone Brochan had worked with both as a Sent One and as a Fallen One. Farrow. She dressed in the white robes of their former comrades and reminded him of Samantha and Rebecca. Soft-spoken. Tenderhearted. Even a bit meek. He couldn't imagine her doing anything worthy of banishment from the skies.

Although she'd fallen from the skies for reasons unknown, she'd never mutated into a beast, as Viola liked to call him. No, Farrow had only grown more beautiful. A mass of black hair tumbled over a light brown shoulder. Lips as red as her crimson wings hid straight pearly whites. Dark, uptilted eyes remained hooded and looked sleepy as if she were forever ready for bed.

"What have you tried since my last visit?" he asked.

"I launched a nuclear bomb here. Not that anyone can tell." She pointed to an unblemished spot on the veil. Maybe she wasn't so tenderhearted and meek, after all. "And your quest? How did it go with your goddess?"

He hesitated to respond. Farrow knew about Viola's key. They kept each other informed on their ideas and errors; the reason Brochan intended to escort her into Nevaeh when he took McCadden. Now he wasn't sure he wished to discuss the goddess with *anyone.*

Ultimately, he grudgingly admitted, "I now have her in my keeping."

She gasped and glided closer. "Does she own a key, as suspected?"

"She does." Why did he feel as if he were betraying Viola? Because of a single kiss? He scoffed at such a ludicrous idea. "She keeps it hidden. For now."

During the shower, Viola had mentioned a temporary truce. A partnership to destroy Midian and Joseph. Brochan was tempted to accept. The two planned bad things for her, and they must be dealt with. Soon.

"I wish to meet her." Excitement pulsed from Farrow. "Perhaps I can convince her to part with the key."

A denial roared inside his head. Viola was *his* prisoner, in *his* fortress, in *his* world. She owed *him*. Her very life depended on his goodwill. And that was just the way he wanted it.

On the other hand, McCadden's life depended on that key.

He grappled with indecision before huffing a breath. "Not yet." He had a plan, and he *would* see it through. "I have set a scheme in motion."

Two or three weeks of isolation, and Narcissism would turn on the goddess. Demons always required a victim. Viola's confidence would crumble. In desperation, she would give Brochan anything he demanded.

He ignored the hot burn of guilt in his chest. "Until its completion," he told Farrow, "we'll hit the veil with everything we've got."

Chapter Six

Viola tiptoed through the fortress, her stomach in knots. Of course, her stomach was never *not* in knots nowadays. Brochan had been absent for an endless eternity! Six days of wretched despair, unrelenting loneliness and frantic worry. Basically, her worst nightmares come to life. Everything she'd battled as a child, times ten.

She'd searched the palace for anyone living or dead and found nothing. Absolutely *nothing*! As a goddess of the Afterlife, she could do things most other deities could not. Feed on souls. Well, she *used* to feed on souls, before her possession. But she could still traverse any plane, see spirits of the dead and communicate with ghosts. To her horror, even the spirits had vacated this realm. No other worlds existed around it, as if the land had been cursed. As if the planet itself had been severed from the highways of the galaxies and left to float across an endless void.

A metaphor for her host's existence?

Or her own?

Tears gathered, blurring her vision. Lonely beyond reason, she'd resorted to uncovering the portraits hanging on the walls just to have people to speak to. Her audience consisted of the stern, painted faces of long-deceased warlocks and witches of old, known by the faint, swirling lines etched across their foreheads.

Viola pulled at the metal cuff Brochan had secured around her wrist. As usual, it didn't budge. Just then, she loathed Brochan with the heat of a thousand suns. How dare he do this to her!? She had no one to speak to but herself. And even though she was stellar company—the best—she couldn't rally her customary confidence. Self-loathing bombarded her daily. And okay, yes, maybe she didn't hate Brochan with the heat of a *thousand* suns. Maybe only a few hundred.

In a secret part of her heart, however, she suspected she only loathed *herself.*

What if she was the worst person ever born? What if the worlds would be better off without her?

Would she die alone as she deserved? Would anyone but Fluffy remember her fondly?

Her friend Cameo might entertain a *few* delightful recollections about her. The first and only friend Viola had made outside of Fluffy. A woman once oppressed by Misery, a demon almost as horrid as Narcissism. Cameo was newly wed to the love of her life, Lazarus, and finally living her happily ever after.

Where's my *happily ever after?* Viola swallowed a sob. She missed her baby so much. Sadness had become an ache in her bones. The perfect complement to the thorn of concern in her brain.

Why hadn't Fluffy flashed to her? The agony of waiting and not knowing. The helplessness of entertaining countless questions without answers. The toll exacted by every rise and crash of emotion.

Her tears spilled down her cheek. She sniffled. Did Brochan feel this way all the time? Wondering when death might sink its claws into his brother. Flayed raw by what could have—should have—been.

Sniffling, she swiped at her damp eyes with a shaky hand. Fact: Brochan treasured his brother. Fact: The beast saw Viola as the cherished male's cruel executioner. Fact: He wasn't exactly wrong.

How could she blame him for treating her poorly? She'd dished much worse to others who'd wronged her. Except, she *did* blame him. She'd done the beast a favor. McCadden had been headed to the front line, where he would have died, losing his immortality *without* Viola's interference. And his life. Her actions had granted him extra time. As a mortal, yes, but extra was extra. He'd never set foot on the battlefield, so he'd avoided a destined death. She should be rewarded for her heroism. Something she'd explained to McCadden. Not that he'd believed her. His mouth-wateringly delicious older brother would be no different.

If her baby suffered…

"Fluffy," she called, her throat wobbly. "Come to Momma." She prayed her words carried to other realms, and he remained strong enough to reach her. *I'll hold him, and everything will be all right.*

She turned a corner, entering another hallway. Sunlight streamed through colored glass, illuminating forgotten side tables and a vase filled with dried, drooping flowers. More portraits covered with dusty cloths hung on the walls. With the change of direction, her thoughts shifted too, sliding from her pet to her captor yet again.

To offer Brochan the use of her beloved body...to *enjoy* herself with a male who didn't like or respect her, a jailer who intended to steal from her... Did she care nothing for her future self?

A magnificent goddess of the Afterlife did *not* succumb to desire for others—others succumbed to their desires for her!

Okay, she was back to hating him. And maybe kinda, sorta sympathizing with him too? Even though Brochan blamed her for his brother's future demise, he'd brought her a new basket of goodies each morning. Fresh breads and cheeses. Jams and honey. Wine. Feasts fit for a queen. Which she didn't understand. Why did he offer gifts at the same time he antagonized her?

Is he as torn as I am?

No, he couldn't be. The rogue had also delivered cleaning supplies and clothing: T-shirts and sweatpants she'd rather die than wear, as well as a French maid costume. The cruel beast obviously taunted her.

She was right the first time. *Definitely hate him.*

When next she caught sight of him, she would tell him. During every delivery, he had somehow remained hidden, as if he'd known when she slumbered, the coast clear. Even though she didn't have a set schedule or know when she would succumb to the need for rest. Did he ever ponder their kiss? Or crave more of her?

A fresh tide of anger frothed. He'd gifted her with the best kiss of her life, the truth of his adoration drowning out the demon's lies. Then he had rejected her. Abandoned her.

He must know what separation from an adoring public did to her. He'd followed her for months. But still, he stayed away?

That settled it. No more kisses for him!

Tremors shook her as she motored forward. When her knees almost buckled, she whimpered. The weakened demon was feeding, weakening *her*. The heartless fiend had even begun revealing those long-buried memories, the terrible truth now so clear...

As she'd smiled and chatted in those recollections, she'd destroyed people with her words. Males and females, mortals and immortals, had withered under her praises. Because her praises were insults!

Scraping noises halted her. Her ears twitched. Did she detect huffing too?

Someone was here!

Gasping, she pressed herself against the nearest wall, hiding in a shadowy corner. Though she was brave—the bravest!—she knew there were times to be leery. This was one such time. She had little strength and few weapons at her disposal.

Had the Forsaken found her? Maybe Brochan had returned for good. Perhaps a stranger had stumbled upon the realm. What if Fluffy had arrived?

Please be Fluffy.

More scraping and huffing, followed by a man's curse. "Just kill me already!"

Definitely not Fluffy. Or Brochan. And yet, she recognized the timbre.

Viola threw a vase to the floor, cringing as the tinkle of shattering glass rang out. After swiping up the largest shard, she raced forward, snaked around another corner and... What?!

"Fluffy!" Relief swamped her as the fur-baby dragged a protesting wolfshifter behind him, teeth clamped firmly around the male's ankle. The one from the bar. "My sweet baby," she cried, lurching closer, bursting with joy.

Her small, wire-haired devampire released his prize. Making the most adorable squeaking sounds, he rushed over and threw himself into her waiting arms.

Careful not to harm him with the glass, Viola rubbed her cheek against his and clutched thirteen pounds of love, beauty and rage to her chest. "I've missed you madly," she told him, her tears flowing freely again.

"You," the shifter said, lumbering to unsteady feet. "You're the one who brought the winged creature to the bar." He evinced worry rather than accusation. "You escaped him. I'm glad."

"I did escape him, yes." For a total of two seconds. To Fluffy, she said, "Did my brilliant darling smell my scent, comprehend my plan, and capture the wolf before flashing here? Who is Mommy's good boy? You are. Yes, yes, you are."

With a weary sigh, her pet rested his head on her shoulder. He, too, had grown weak. Weaker than before. Had he suffered without her?

She bit the inside of her cheek to silence a whimper. Fluffy required an infusion of immortality, and he needed it now. There was no time to charm the wolf. "I'm Viola, goddess of the Afterlife," she announced, meeting his gaze head-on. "One of many, but by far the best. I see auras, and yours tells me that you're going to die. Soon." Before, the glowing outline around him had contained striations of black. Now, a black aura contained striations of red and gray, the little cracks caused by fury and sadness. The two emotions had worked together, draining his strength as swiftly as Narcissism had drained hers. "Death courts you even now."

"It does?" To her amazement, he dropped to his knees and smiled. "Finally, I will join my mate."

Ohhhh. He was one of *those*. The rarest, sweetest fruit in existence. A fated mate willing himself to die, eager to be with a slain lover again. Although, his lifeforce must be weaker than it appeared. Weak, yes, but viable. At the very least, he would recharge Fluffy's battery, buying more time. Months, maybe. Besides, such loyalty deserved a reward. Viola could help him *and* her baby.

"You plan to escort my spirit to the hereafter?" he asked, more eager by the minute. Admiring, maybe. Oh, yes. Admiring *definitely*.

She jolted, her eyes widening. That admiration hit her with the potency of high-octane fuel. Strength flooded her as if a dam had crumbled. Mmm. Delicious.

This shifter might be the answer to her every problem. "There'll be no escorting. I plan to…accept the gift of your immortality." Why not be blunt? "You'll become human and die faster. All I need is your agreement."

"Yes. You have it. Agreed. Accepted. Whatever declaration you need to hear." He shot to his feet and tripped her way, his eagerness palpable, his admiration greater. "Take my immortality. Take it now."

Wow. Convincing a man to part with his lifeforce had never been easier.

After kissing Fluffy's precious little snout, she eased him to the floor, where he settled. She straightened and focused on her new best friend, the wolfshifter. "Shall we begin?"

"I'm wondering why we haven't started already," he said, stepping closer. "What do you need me to do?"

"Resist the urge to fight me when the pain comes." With the cuff on her wrist, she couldn't do this the easy way. Meaning, she couldn't dematerialize into spirit form to reach inside his body and carefully sever the heart of his immortality from his spirit. She had to go old school.

Viola erased the rest of the distance and planted her hands on his shoulders. He tensed, but he didn't issue a protest. She drew in a deep breath, her mind whirling. In seconds, she would end his life. *Another death stain on my soul.* A temporary fix for her troubles, and another action for Narcissism to use against her.

But what other choice did she have?

A long-forgotten part of her whispered, *There's always another way.*

Maybe truth, maybe not. Either way, she could see no other road to travel. "Thank you for your sacrifice, wolf." Viola offered him a half-hearted smile before pressing her mouth against his.

He exhaled a puff of air, his lips parting. Excellent. She inhaled sharply, stealing the breath and forcing the heart of his immortality to ascend from his innermost being.

He grunted an agonized sound, but he didn't attempt to sever contact. She sucked harder and faster until a small ball of muted light floated from him. The weaker the lifeforce, the duller the glow.

With this, Fluffy might gain a month, but no more. No matter. They had time now. Other donors could be found and brought here as necessary.

Once Viola swallowed the muted light, separating it from the shifter, she released his shoulders. He collapsed, alive but fading fast. Warmth spread through her belly as she knelt by Fluffy and placed her mouth before his. Deep inhale. Slow but formidable exhale. Because the beam wasn't yet tethered to any part of her, it rose with ease, leaving her to flow into the animal's open mouth.

As soon as the process completed, Fluffy smiled and jumped to his feet. Happy to be alive and strong again, he raced from one end of the hall to the other, then back. How adorable. He had the zoomies.

Fresh relief inundated Viola. She returned her attention to the shifter, who observed her curiously from his spot on the floor.

"Thank you," he croaked. The adoration in his dark, puppy-dog eyes had intensified.

She *must* be amazing. Look at how much she'd helped him.

Tendrils of strength unfurled in her limbs, and they were far stronger than the first. Her tremors ceased. How wondrous! No one had ever thanked her for this act. Most often, she'd received exclamations of regret and demands for a reversal.

"Thank *you*," she said, and she meant it. "Your kindness has brought me great joy." If only she could reward him. Mark him to ensure he remained protected in the spirit realm. The cuff ruined everything.

Including her outfit: the white dress she'd washed in the bathroom sink. "One day, I'll find your spirit. I'll help you in some way. I vow it."

She might forget the vow for a few centuries, but she would remember eventually.

With his last breath, the shifter rasped, "You have helped me already, goddess. I go to find my girl." His gaze deadened, staring at nothing as his head lolled to the side.

Viola blinked away tears of…guilt? Relief? Whatever. Emotions had to wait. "Flash Mommy home," she said to Fluffy. Something he'd done on more than one occasion.

Her baby leaped into her arms. Seconds passed, but nothing happened. Her pet grew agitated, and she frowned.

"The cuff," she grated. "It must prevent anyone but Brochan from flashing me." Well, she needed to deal with her beast, anyway. Now, at least, she had the strength to do so.

Forcing a bright smile for her pet's peace of mind, she set Fluffy on his feet and stood. "Return the body to the bar, my darling. Then fetch Mommy's go-bag." A duffel filled with weapons, weapons and more weapons. Brochan had confiscated her jewelry during one of his visits.

While he was gone, she could change and—gag—clean a room or two. Fluffy deserved to stay in a luxurious palace, not some musty hovel. When Brochan returned, she might offer the beast a final chance to work with her to eradicate the Forsaken who threatened her wellbeing. If he refused a second time… She might do to him what she'd done to the shifter, a poisonous Forsaken or not.

Viola regarded the metal wrist cuff. Desperate measures would be taken.

* * * *

Brochan drew in a breath and braced for impact. He held an unconscious Sent One against his chest. A male he'd never met. A soldier he'd plucked from the skies only minutes ago.

He hovered a mile from the veil, his wings gliding up and down. Farrow remained at his side. She, too, held an unconscious Sent One.

She nodded at Brochan. "I'm ready."

"On three," he told her. "One. Two. Now!" He flapped his wings with more vigor and jetted forward. A living arrow.

Farrow kept pace beside him. They sped toward the veil, faster and faster, building momentum, expecting to bypass the invisible barrier with the Sent Ones they held.

Closer…

Mere seconds away…

Impact! Brochan ricocheted back, his bones breaking, and his organs reduced to pulp. The Sent One soared through, skidding over the lush green grass. Farrow's Sent One rolled beside him.

Pain registered as blood dripped into his eyes, blurring his vision. By sheer will alone, he caught himself in the sky. Farrow labored to his side, a wing twisted at an odd angle. Gashes littered her face.

Guilt pricked him. "Another failure," he said, swiping his tongue over his teeth. He stiffened as a sense of rising trepidation rippled across the bond he shared with his brother.

McCadden! "My brother needs me." He flashed to the bottom floor of the Downfall, not bothering with niceties outside. The club's walls materialized around him, revealing a raging battle in every direction. A horde of Forsaken had invaded.

Midian had kept his promise and now fought to acquire McCadden, in order to bargain for Viola.

The scarred Xerxes stood with the blond Thane and the bronze Bjorn, forming a circle. The trio killed Forsaken savagely, using swords of fire to strike. Like machines, they maimed their foes in a continuous stream, and they did it all while staying in place. Their golden wings spread wide to encompass the tattooed, pink haired McCadden and several females, creating an impenetrable shield the enemy couldn't breach.

Farrow appeared at Brochan's side, taking stock in seconds.

Merciless, Brochan threw himself into the fray, raking his claws and brand-new wing joints over anyone within reach. Soldiers dropped, sometimes three at a time, piling around him. He latched onto his next victim and ripped off the male's head. Icy black blood spurted, spraying him.

What would his mate think of him now?

No thoughts of the goddess. One always led to a second and a third, fourth, fifth, until he considered nothing but returning to her. And she wasn't his mate.

With a roar and a ram of his horns, he took out the next two— three—soldiers. He slashed and clawed. He shredded. But even still, he failed to boot the goddess from his mind. Why hadn't he kissed and touched her while he'd had the chance? Why hadn't he enjoyed her while she was warm and pliant?

Because I want her to want me as intensely as I want her, not because she thinks to use me.

Had her confidence crumbled yet? He wasn't sure he could remain separated from her another week, much less another day. As soon as he'd sensed her deep slumber, he had checked on her. She'd never fallen asleep in the same location, had always huddled in a semi-secure spot. Behind a wall, after crawling past broken slats. A cubby hole in the floor. A beam anchored to the ceiling.

How small and fragile she'd seemed yesterday. The urge to curl up beside her had nearly overwhelmed him. Every day, she'd grown a little paler. Dark shadows had taken up permanent residence under her eyes. Her misery brought him no delight. Guilt did more than prick him—it gouged him.

Brochan's gaze caught on McCadden, who witnessed the worst of his fury through a gap between Thane's and Xerxes' wings. His brother conveyed horror.

Brochan flushed as he assassinated the next flood of soldiers. Beside him, Farrow brutalized her opponents.

Like other Forsaken, he'd lost the ability to produce a sword of fire. Not Farrow. Though her ability had mutated, the sword becoming a grotesque whip. Thousands of teeth protruded from hundreds of tentacles braided together. As she swung her arm, the whip's handle appeared in her grip. Tentacles lashed out, wrapping around different parts of a Forsaken, binding his wings and arms to his body and cinching his legs together, choking him until his head simply popped off.

Finally, only a handful of Forsaken remained, Midian and Joseph among them. Brochan's gaze collided with Midian's as he drove one set of claws into a warrior's skull and burrowed the other into the male's throat. With one fluid motion, Brochan ripped off his opponent's head.

"This isn't the end," Midian spat just before he vanished. The other Forsaken retreated, following after him.

Brochan and those on his side lingered, on alert for a counterattack. Minutes passed without incident. He realized he still held the severed head. A head hissing curses, much to the shock of the Sent Ones and those they guarded.

"Burn the bodies. Burn everything," he commanded. "Let's find out if a Forsaken can truly revive from any death." If not, perhaps a certain goddess of the Afterlife could do the deed.

Anticipation overshadowed his remaining fury, and he balled his free hand into a fist. Should he question her before she fell asleep?

As the Sent Ones ushered their charges far from the carnage, the bonding tattoo on Brochan's arm heated. No, it was already hot. His burst of adrenaline had muted the mark's power. Now, with the fighting over, Viola's emotions inundated him, and he frowned. Fear? Excitement? He couldn't tell.

"I must go," he shouted at the others, then flashed to the fortress to confront his goddess.

Chapter Seven

Viola sang a ballad with the most beautiful voice in the history of beautiful voices as she scrubbed the master bedroom she planned to (secretly) share with Fluffy, who had yet to return from his errand. For once, however, she didn't mind being alone. Not much, anyway.

With her worries eclipsed by expectancy, Narcissism had no ammunition to use against her and remained blessedly quiet. She'd even plotted a rock-solid strategy to deal with Brochan. Get this. When he returned home, Viola would ignore him. The worst punishment she could dish. Why, if he appeared right this second, she'd look straight through him.

So this idea had failed in the past, allowing other males to pretend they didn't care, turning the tables on her. So what? Brochan would froth at the mouth, desperate to re-enter her good graces.

"What is that racket? What are you doing?" The questions thundered through the room, and she gasped, meeting the Forsaken's gaze over her shoulder. He looked her over, his frown deepening. "You're on your knees. Cleaning. Wearing the costume and a thong. And heels." The storm faded from his expression, leaving incredulity. He swallowed, his Adam's apple bobbing.

Her stomach twisted as she threw her rag into the bucket of soapy water and scrambled to her feet, facing him. *Oh, my.* He appeared...*wow.* He was shirtless, his leathers hanging low on his waist, and ripped in several places. Black blood splattered bulging muscles and the tattoo on his forearm—crisscrossing lines and scattered dots.

He heaved his breaths and clasped a severed head. A talking head, dripping death onto her clean floor.

With a screech, she stomped her foot. "You fiend!" Forget ignoring him. "You're ruining my floor. I scrubbed for *minutes,* and you dirtied it all in seconds. I'll never forgive you for this. Never!" Her tirade downgraded to haughty acceptance in an instant. She wasn't alone anymore! "Also, I adore the gift, and I humbly accept it as my due. Shall we display it on my mantel?"

The furrows in his brow conquered new ground. He cast his gaze to the head dangling from his grip and cringed. "You're cleaning," he said, focusing on her again. "In costume."

His astonishment proved she'd made a lasting impression. "Yes. I donned the French maid outfit to do my chores." She'd even anchored her mass of pale hair into a bun. "The other option was sweatpants, but I think we can both agree I don't have the erectile bulge to pull those off."

"You're..." His eyes widened as he perused her once again...only slower. He gulped at the bodice and licked his lips at the mid-thigh ruffles. "You..."

Viola savored a swell of strength and pleasure. Mmm. Another dose of pure, undiluted adoration. How she'd missed it. "I'm magnificent? Perfection? Trust me, *I know.*" She heaved a mournful sigh. "But that's my burden to carry. Something few others can comprehend. As for you..."

As she gave him an equally unhurried examination, she noted a stronger awareness of *Brochan's* appeal. Such aggressive masculinity. An intensity she'd never encountered from another. With his wings partially flared, and his free hand fisted, he exuded barely banked ferocity.

As she continued to look him over, he bowed up. Expecting her to insult him?

"I don't care to hear what you think of me. I want to know what brought about this change in you, and I want to know now." The statements lashed like a whip. "Yesterday, you were sad. Weakening. Today, you're happy. Strong. Why?"

Careful. Reveal nothing. But, uh, how did he know the state of her emotions, exactly? "Perhaps I remembered your great desire for me. Maybe there's another reason. Either way, I won't discuss *anything* with a male in the process of ruining my floor. Especially the area I intended to consider scrubbing next."

His eyes slitted. "You have one hour. I will return, and you will give me the answers I seek. Be ready."

"You're leaving me again?" Her pulse leaped, panic surging without delay. Thankfully, she tamped it down swiftly and schooled her features to reveal disdain. "Well, good riddance. I don't care what you do. Never have, never will."

A scowling Brochan flashed away, and Viola sagged.

The too-brief interaction rolled over and over in her mind. What did he wish to discuss? The key? The ways he planned to torture her? All the amazing things he'd missed about her?

What did she want from him again? His sudden appearance had wiped her final resolution from her mind.

Whatever she decided, she must prepare quickly. Viola needed to condense six hours of primping into sixty minutes.

She flew into the bathroom and hurried through a shower, pretending the toiletries didn't smell like Brochan, and her blood didn't heat with every inhalation. She dried and styled her hair, then strode into the closet, expecting to find an array of tops with holes and ties in the back, all sized giant. She'd been wearing Brochan's shirts as dresses.

Wait. New garments hung from hangers. Gowns of every color and style. Silks, satins, and velvets. Her heart about melted with joy. Where had her host found these beauties worthy of a queen?

She selected a lovely dress with fabric the same silvery hue as the Forsaken's eyes. The silk molded to her curves, leaving an indecent amount of cleavage. The hem reached the floor, high slits providing mobility. The awful cuff acted as her only piece of jewelry.

Well, well. Brochan *forgot* to provide underwear. How interesting. He must have—

Viola sensed him before she saw him, his heat setting her nerve endings on fire. She spun, and there he stood, only a few feet away from her. He'd showered also. Thankfully, he'd deposited the decapitated head somewhere else. Locks of damp hair clung to his brow, his cheeks. He wore a plain white T-shirt and black leather pants. Still no combat boots.

He was…beautiful. And he was gaping at her.

Deluged with power, she preened at him. She deemed his reaction appropriate. "Allow me to articulate what you're currently feeling, beast. Your entire world has shifted, the sight of me burned into your memory forevermore."

He gulped, nodded, and took her hand, his rough palm tickling her skin. He led her to the balcony, where he shouldered open the double doors. A cool breeze rushed in, enveloping her with a chill until he tugged her in front of him, putting her chest flush against his.

"Hold tight," he commanded, wrapping his strong arms around her. Flaring his wings and flinging water droplets in every direction, he shot into the air.

Wind combed through her hair as she clung to him. "Where are we going?" she asked, nervous but excited. She'd never flown in the shelter of anyone's arms before.

The most wonderful heat enveloped her, infused with Brochan's heady male scent. His strength charged her up as surely as the wolf's admiration.

"An oasis sprang up the day after you used the faucet." He rolled through a fluffy white cloud, soared over a barren hill, and began his descent.

She almost huffed with disappointment. Over so soon?

When he landed, he set her on her feet. But he didn't release her, and she didn't step back. His gaze searched hers as he traced his hands up the ridges of her spine before massaging her nape.

Deep yearning seeped from him. Fury, too. All that barely banked ferocity rippled through his wings, and she battled a strange urge to comfort him. To hold him and never let go.

The urge to kiss him bombarded her next, and Viola jumped back at last, least she give in.

Kiss her captor before he groveled for forgiveness? No. Besides, they needed to nail down some of the finer details of their relationship. For six days, he'd kept her isolated, on edge and miserable. He continued to threaten her pet and blame her for his brother's condition. He hadn't *earned* a kiss yet.

She turned on her heel. The cut direct. And she wouldn't feel bad about it! Not even when she later replayed the flash of hurt she'd briefly spied in his expression.

As promised, an oasis stretched before her. Miles and miles of lush, emerald foliage teeming with pink and yellow blooms stole her breath. Butterflies the size of her fist perched here and there. A jungle worthy of a goddess.

Viola skipped forward to smell a flower. A warrior wouldn't reward a despised enemy with such a prize. But he might bring a female he hoped to bed...

Brochan followed, staying close to her heels. "This isn't a candlelit dinner, I know," he told her begrudgingly. Reluctantly. "I hope it's better."

Much. "Is this our first date?" she gasped, pressing a hand over her thumping heart.

He scrubbed his too-harsh features. "This is a temporary truce."

* * * *

"Are you sure it isn't a date?" Viola asked, batting her lashes at him. "I mean, if it looks like a date and acts like a date…"

Brochan ground his teeth. "A date comes with hope for a future together." *And you do not have a future with your mate?*

She's not my mate.

"And passion," she quipped.

He closed his eyes for a moment, searching for calm. *Just get this done.*

With great reluctance and an undeniable sliver of eagerness, he slid an arm around her waist, urging her forward. As they walked side by side, unease prickled the back of his neck. She was a powerful goddess of the Afterlife, and she wielded a unique set of skills. Abilities to kill the unkillable. Dangerous talents she could use against Brochan once she finished off Midian and Joseph.

For McCadden, however, Brochan would risk anything.

Soft foliage seemed to lean into her and away from him. He looked up. Anywhere but at his companion. A tier of small suns dominated one side of a lavender sky, beaming streaks of gold.

"How did you find this place?" she asked.

A safe topic. He breathed easier. "As a Sent One, I hunted a rogue horde of Wrath's minions here." Lowborn demons who served a higher-ranked master. "This was once a thriving fae realm. But the citizens listened to the evil whispers of the demons and caved to their wicked influence, soon destroying their world and each other. By the time I slaughtered the final minions, only this wasteland remained."

"Ah. I know those evil whispers well."

He supposed she did. "Why were you chosen to host Narcissism?"

A moment passed in silence before she sighed. "I'd already unlocked a door and hung a flashing neon sign that read *Demons Drink for Free!*"

He understood her reference. A single mind was vaster than any galaxy, filled with countless doors, pathways and portals, each one leading to untold delights…or horrors. But no demon could enter a mind without permission from its owner, whether that permission came wittingly or unwittingly. Permission came through thoughts and emotions, for thoughts and emotions kept the doors, pathways and portals sealed, or held them wide open.

"Which emotion did the demon attach to?" he asked.

"Insecurity. What else?"

That, he couldn't comprehend. "You? Insecure?"

Another moment passed in silence. "By the way," she said, "the oasis didn't pop up because of the faucet."

Though he was disappointed, he allowed the subject change without comment. "Why did it pop up, then?"

She traced her fingertips over a leaf. "The world is thanking me for visiting, bringing beauty, peace and love. As well as the harshest discipline if ever my wishes are disobeyed. And I accept," she called, spreading her arms.

New flowers bloomed, as if to prove her claim.

He didn't want to be charmed by this, by her, but... He was undeniably charmed.

"Are we in the middle of a truce?" she asked. "I need to hear you say the words."

"We...are."

"Excellent." She gripped his arm with one hand and pointed to somewhere high up with the other. "I must have it. As my ally, you're obligated to fetch it for me."

The touch, slight though it was, scorched him. Heart thumping, he followed the line of her outstretched finger but found nothing extraordinary. "What must I fetch, goddess?" Whatever it was, he would acquire it, no matter the labor involved. Because...just because. He didn't need to explain himself to anyone, least of all himself!

"The cherry-red fruit high, high in the tree. See?" She turned her body into his and batted her lashes at him. Sunlight bathed her flawless features, painting her flesh with a golden glow. "Pluck it for me. Help satisfy my hunger."

He gulped. Such wonder for a piece of fruit? Helpless to resist her—in this, only this—he flared his wings and flew up, reaching out.

"Not that one," she called. "No, not that one, either. Nope. Nope. Brochan, were you even listening to me when I described the object of my desire? I said cherry-red, not merlot, scarlet, apple or garnet. No, not sangria or currant, either. Yes! That's it. That's the one."

She certainly knew what she wanted. He'd always admired that about her. A trait he'd noticed right away. She'd locked her gaze on McCadden and never deviated. Until she'd won him.

Scowling, Brochan plucked the fruit as directed, then floated to his feet and offered her the gift.

With a blindingly bright smile, she accepted and peeled the skin, revealing plump, silvery berries sectioned by a large pit. "They're the same color as your eyes. So pretty."

His scowl melted away as he blinked. "You like my eyes?"

"Very much." To his surprise, she offered the first berry to him, a payment of sorts.

Poison? Did he care? As he opened, unable to resist temptation, she placed the fruit upon his tongue. He closed his mouth around her fingers and sucked, sweetness awakening his taste buds.

Her pupils expanded, and her lips parted. Then she chuckled. "Naughty beast."

Muscles clenched in reflex. The need to sweep her into his arms threatened to unman him. Everything about this woman seduced him. As if she were made for him.

What if she *was* his mate?

He gnashed his molars. How many others had felt this way about her?

"If you could have any woman," she said as they continued their stroll, sharing and finishing the fruit, "who is it, and why is it me? I expect to hear the top three reasons. Minimum."

He should deny her assumption. If he did, he would be lying. Only cowards lied.

Focus on anything else. "How did you occupy your time this week?"

Like him, she allowed a subject change without protest. "The same way you did, I'm sure. Imagining all the things you wished you'd done to me while I showered."

The bluntly stated truth nailed him straight in the gut. "Cease attempting to garner softer emotions from me, goddess. Be honest with me for once."

"I am honest with you always, Brochan." Wink. "Always sometimes."

This playful side of her unnerved him, reminding him of a thousand other questions he'd entertained since his return. Where was her sadness? Her worry for her beloved pet? Or had she abandoned him, too?

"Why did you begin cleaning the bedchamber today?" he asked harsher than intended. She'd done it the same day she'd experienced a burst of excitement. That wasn't a coincidence. Something had happened.

"Why does it matter? You abandoned me," she said, each word hardening. "You wanted me weak so I'd willingly bargain away the key."

Shame attempted to spark. *Ignore.* "Yet you strengthened. How?"

Smug, she flipped her hair. "Maybe I fell in love with myself again. You've met me, right? We can both agree no one's more admirable."

"Or sexier," he grumbled without thought. His cheeks heated. Perhaps she hadn't heard—

She darted in front of him and twirled into him, forcing him to stop and grab her, lest his big body fling hers to the ground. "I *knew* you craved me!"

"That isn't what I said."

"But it's what you meant."

Probably. How well she fit his grip. "Do you wish to hear my admission? Very well. Give me the key you aren't using, and I'll describe every sordid fantasy I've ever had about you."

With a roll of her eyes, she said, "First of all, you'll describe every sordid fantasy no matter what. You won't be able to help yourself. Second, who says I'm not using the key? For your information, I like to maintain an escape pad from my legion of admirers."

"Give me the key, save McCadden's life, and I'll cancel your debt to me."

She jerked, panic seeping from her before she settled down, acting as if nothing odd had occurred.

"I'll cease following you, you have my vow," he told her, even as his instincts protested. Not see her again? Not protect her from other threats?

"Why would I ever part with such a dedicated stalker?" she asked, seeming sincere. "The more admirers the better, I always say."

"Only moments ago, you claimed you wished to *escape* your legion of admirers," he grated.

"So? I don't have to be logical or consistent to be accurate."

His molars nearly ground into powder. But his irritation didn't last long. Why torture himself? Why not enjoy the truce while he could?

Sighing, Brochan swooped her into his arms. Without hesitation, she rested her head on his shoulder, settling in. The softness of her skin scrambled his brain as he carried her to the mouth of a large cave, teeming with sprigs of pink flowers.

"You may not have a key to Nevaeh," she said, toying with his earlobe, "but you do have a ticket to paradise."

The sky opened without warning and showered rain upon the oasis.

Leaping and twirling to the center of the cave ledge as if it were her stage, Viola mesmerized him. Laughter spilled from her. The kind of laughter he hadn't heard since his days in the uppermost level of the skies. Genuine and undiluted by sadness. This female enjoyed life in a way he never had.

"Why would you ever wish to leave this place?" she asked.

His chest cracked, and he lost his breath. "I seek a land without time, where McCadden will never grow old. I've yet to find one like Nevaeh."

Viola pursed her lips. "Does he *want* to live forever?"

"Of course, he does." What kind of foolish question was that? "I *must* get him into Nevaeh, Viola. He was only three years old when our parents deemed him tainted. They kicked him from our home, breaking his fragile heart. I was fifteen at the time. I moved out and took over his care, doing my best to provide everything he needed." An action Brochan had never regretted.

The color drained from her cheeks, leaving her pallid. "I see."

"Do you?"

"I do." She flattened her hands over her stomach. "He is your beloved child."

Perhaps she did see. Some of the tension loosened in his chest. "Yes. He is my child in every way that matters." Brochan stalked past her, taking shelter inside the cave while keeping the goddess in his sights.

Raindrops continued sluicing down her lush curves, soaking her dress, reminding him of her shower.

His tension returned, worse than before. Brochan dropped his chin, laser-focused on his companion. "Give me the key, goddess."

* * * *

The rain pitter-pattered, and Viola's happy buzz faded. Brochan sure did know how to ruin a moment. He wouldn't be too thrilled when he learned the truth about the nonexistent key. He might even feel as if he'd lost his only family yet again.

Inside, she cringed. As a mother, how could she hurt a father?

What if she found another way to save McCadden? She'd rescued Fluffy from the jaws of death using a literal piece of her heart. A pinch she'd severed from herself and wove into his—a spiritual process she'd learned from books.

If Viola shared a piece of herself with McCadden, she would need to feed him the same way she fed Fluffy. Her heart wasn't a natural part of his, and it would drain, requiring charging.

"Give me what I want," Brochan said. "I...I'm willing to partner with you to permanently neutralize the other Forsaken."

"Wait. Hold up. In this so-called partnership, you get deliverance from your foes *and* a key?" Just not the one he assumed. "What do I get?" She plucked a flower and nestled its soft petals against her cheek before weaving the bloom into her hair.

"You receive deliverance from your foes as well. *And* freedom," he grated. "Do you agree or not, goddess?"

"Not!" Giddy—ruthless—she peered at him over her shoulder. She'd won. Mostly. Kill the Forsaken, her enemies, and Brochan allowed her to feed Fluffy without interference? Done. "I demand a vow of eternal protection. Consider it a captivity tax. That's my deal. Take it or leave it."

His nostrils flared. "Sent Ones only bestow vows of eternal protection to their mates."

"Good thing you aren't a Sent One then. Although, there's a slight chance I could be convinced to possibly consider pondering a long-term union with you." Why not? If he were the one to pass her test...

A huff of irritation. "Stop pretending to desire me, Viola."

Something about his tone and defensive posture unsettled her. She considered his display of vulnerability in the shower stall. How he'd flushed when they'd discussed lovemaking. How his previous partners had turned their heads, avoiding his kiss. Deflating his pride.

I can build his confidence.

When you can't even build your own? The demon laughed at her.

She cringed as if the fiend had struck her. Rephrase. She *wanted* to build Brochan's confidence. Since they were partners, she should try.

Yes. Aid him now, destroy him later. Good plan.

Viola jerked, then tried to hide the action by pretending to sniff another bloom. "Brochan, if you can't tell when I'm being genuine or not, that's on you. Now. If you'd like access to my key, you'll give me one hour of devotion a day. At least." Though he continued to deny it, he yearned for her as much as she yearned for him. He must. All he lacked was an excuse to give in.

Happy to oblige, darling. For the first time in a long time, a male intrigued her. Why not explore their connection while she had the chance?

Facing him fully, she said, "Do *you* agree, beast?"

A strangled sound left him. "You're trying to manage me again."

In part, yes. But she also kind of loved how this male made her feel, and she only wanted more. Still, she forced a shrug. "Let's return to our old bargain, then. You stay away from me, and I tell you nothing."

He ran his tongue over his straight, white teeth. "Nothing you do will change my opinion of you. And I won't bed you."

She offered her most cutting smile. "I don't recall asking you to bed me."

His nostrils flared. Okay, so her first efforts to boost his confidence had just crashed and burned. Not her fault. His.

"You think you'll enjoy this," he hissed at her. "I look forward to proving you wrong."

Tipping an invisible hat to him, she said, "My very best to you, sir. Your efforts will end in failure, but at least you will have tried, right?"

He worked his jaw. To her surprise, he snapped, "I agree to your terms, goddess. Just know that I will detest every moment we're together."

Doubtful. She heard his crackle of anticipation. She even felt a change in the atmosphere. An electric charge of excitement.

Triumph should have detonated. A glitter bomb of satisfaction. She had won this round. Just as she would win every round. But she merely experienced her own anticipation...

"Why wait?" she asked. "I'm ready for my devotion now."

"You will answer my questions first." He crossed his arms over his chest. "How long have you owned the key?"

Careful. "As long as I can remember."

"Have you ever permitted others to use it?"

A pang of sadness sliced her insides to ribbons. "Far too often," she admitted. The men she'd cared for had enjoyed her greatly...for a short period of time.

Why did the people in her life leave her? How did they not recognize her incredible worth?

"How did you get the key?" Brochan asked.

"My mother and father gave it to me." Another honest but misleading response. "Look. I get why you want McCadden in a timeless land. But why do the other Forsaken wish to return?"

"For my kind, it's a need. An uncontrollable pull." He scoured a hand through his hair, tension tightening his expression. "Why did you choose McCadden?"

Not a subject she enjoyed. "I told you why," she replied softly, gently. "But you called me a liar."

"Because he was soon to die? No." A clipped shake of his head. "You can do many things, goddess, but you cannot predict when another will pass. You are powerful, but you aren't an oracle."

"And thank goodness for that! Oracles are the absolute *worst,* always dishing out puzzles with only half the pieces, inciting self-fulfilled prophecies of doom. But as a goddess of the Afterlife, I'm attuned to…say it with me. *The Afterlife.* I read auras."

She moved to another bloom and peeked at her winged warrior through the thick shield of her lashes. No signs of softening yet.

Trying again. "I choose men who are either soon to die or those I might be able to fall in love with. Bonus points if one is both, and I'm able to save him from the jaws of death." To be a real family? To belong to someone else. Someone who understood her and her challenges—she had all the best ones! "I do want a male of my own, Brochan. Very much." Did she have a fated one?

No reaction from her companion.

Motoring on. "I win hearts with flirtations and smiles, then test loyalties. When the males fail—and they always fail—I accept their immortality as payment for my time."

He stretched his fingers, then curled them in once again. "Your time is more valuable than theirs?"

"Yes. No. My reasons made sense once." She offered him a sad smile, the fight evaporating from her. This man had put her through the wringer lately. She longed for peace. "I wasn't raised around people. I spent my childhood locked inside a home, hidden. Soon after I broke free, I was imprisoned in Tartarus for the most treacherous of reasons—and not my own. I learned to count on myself long before Narcissism entered the picture." The admissions tumbled from her lips, and she couldn't stop them. *What is this male doing to me?* She hurried to change the subject before he responded to her uncharacteristic openness. "Tell me about your former lovers. The two who turned from your kisses."

Though his cheeks reddened, he kept his gaze on her, expression curious and…she wasn't sure. The emotion bothered her, whatever it was.

He drew his wings closer. "At eighteen, I let a council of Sent Ones select a wife for me. A mother for McCadden."

He'd married? Jealousy sparked, and she bit her cheek. "Go on."

"I didn't know it at the time, but Samantha esteemed another. Eventually, she divorced me to wed him. Rebecca left me for reasons unknown." A muscle jumped beneath his eye. "Perhaps she merely wished to escape my *hideous face*."

Ouch. Okay. Viola had thrown the insult to hurt him. Because yes, he had hurt her. Retaliation was supposed to make her feel better, not worse.

She forged ahead, the prize worth the effort. "I happen to like your face." Truth. "And I have the best taste in the history of taste. Ask anyone."

He pursed his lips, far from mollified. "I'm the only person available to admire you. Of course you like my face right now."

As she peered over at her captor…her partner…the male she desired, with his harsh features, rough demeanor, and dignity of a merciless king, Viola came to a startling decision. She wanted more than her own enjoyment—she wanted his. And not only to prove a point.

"Why are you peering at me like that?" he demanded, growing as stiff as a board.

"Like what?" Strolling toward him, she rasped, "Like I want to *show* you how handsome you are?"

Chapter Eight

Brochan watched, enthralled, as his goddess crossed the distance between them, a vision in her silvery gown. Her eyes were hooded, her red lips parted. Long, blond hair swayed with her every movement. Each step separated the slits in her damp skirt, revealing more of her perfect legs.

With the foliage and flowers behind her, her whiskey eyes glittering, she might as well have stepped from a dream.

He groused, "I'm not going to harm you, Viola. You don't have to pretend to desire me."

"I thought we covered this already." She stopped in front of him. The rain had rendered the fabric of her dress transparent. "I'm not pretending."

Muscles clenched on bone, his body aching. *Pure temptation…*

Look away! "You didn't want me before this." Pouting and complaining rather than stating a simple fact? Very well. "When we kissed, you got lost in your head." Exactly as Samantha and Rebecca used to do when he touched them.

"Why *wouldn't* I get lost in my head? I was making out with the guy determined to kill me. I had qualms."

Ohhh. Air deflated from his lungs, shock tossing him into a tailspin. And he'd already been spinning, thunderstruck by the childhood memories she'd shared. The suffering she'd endured. The pain he'd detected had nearly rent him in two, a need to defend her rising. To protect and comfort.

Defend, protect and comfort McCadden's would-be killer? No. But give her an hour of devotion each day? That he could—should—do.

There was no better method to keep her docile.

"Brochan?"

What would she request now? "Yes, Viola?"

"My demonstration of your handsomeness requires repositioning for both of us. Sit." Cupping his shoulders, she urged him to the ground.

He offered no resistance as she eased upon his lap. A slight weight, and yet he felt her in every cell of his body. His heart raced. "What do you hope to accomplish with this, goddess?"

"Many things."

"List the top five." His hands sought her of their own accord, one landing on each side of her waist. The sight of his claws resting against her delicate form struck him as obscene. Heat blistered his cheeks as he pried his fingers free, one by one.

"Only the top five? How you limit me." Just before he eliminated contact completely, she clasped his wrists, holding him in place, and offered her softest smile. "Perhaps there is a reason that supersedes all others. Perhaps I seek...satisfaction."

His entire body jerked. "And you think you can find satisfaction with me?"

"I do."

How much he yearned to believe her. Experience had taught him better.

"Stop thinking. This is supposed to be fun, not torture." She leaned into him and gently pressed her lips to his. "Relax a little."

Fun? Had he *ever* had fun? In the skies, he'd gone from training to be a warrior, to parenting his younger brother to fighting in the Sent One army, to falling, to morphing into a monster brimming with hatred and revenge.

Revenge. Yes. He should oversee his. And yet...any thoughts of his brother faded. Brochan grasped for them, desperate to maintain some sort of defense against this woman's powerful allure.

"Can you guess what comes next?" She brushed the tip of her nose against his.

He gave a clipped shake of his head. "Tell me what to do."

Holding his gaze, Viola asked, "What did you imagine doing to me in the shower?"

Everything.

A little chuckle left her, as if she'd read his mind. "I have another question for you, which will be followed by a request. What you do afterward is up to you. Are you ready? Where did—do—you want to touch me first? Wherever it is, you have my permission to do so…"

He gulped, his thoughts tumbling over each other. What he should choose. Why he should choose it. What she might desire herself. But honestly? There was one place he wished to touch more than any other. So…

He did it. Brochan reached up and cupped her jawline, tracing his thumbs over her cheek bones.

Her pupils exploded over her irises, and her lips parted. She blinked rapidly, layers of her calm disintegrating before his eyes until only vulnerability remained. "I don't understand. You can select any part of me and you start there? Why?"

"Because I can." Because she wasn't just a body to him, even though he wished she were.

"Oh." Eyes wide, she nuzzled his palms. "Where do you wish to touch me next?"

Brochan glided his fingertips to her bare shoulders. The softness of her skin turned the innocent action into brutally erotic caresses, and he nearly roared. His breaths grew labored, the air around him—around *them*—growing thicker.

"Where else?" she asked with a thick voice, tilting her head to bare the elegant expanse of her throat. Making a suggestion?

He licked his lips, staring at her racing pulse. *I'll only touch her there. I won't lick. I'll resist my needs. Will resist…*

Brochan leaned forward and glided his tongue over the spot. The barest flick, and yet she moaned in response. Music to his ears.

His aches…agonizing. Consuming. Here. There. Everywhere. Sweat broke out on his brow as he bent his knees, forcing her closer to him. The added pressure nearly fractured his resolve. He'd wanted this to be about her, only her, and yet…

"Beast," she breathed, as if the description were the sweetest endearment.

The fractures spread…resistance shattered. He flipped her onto her back swiftly, catching her and easing her to the ground softly, then rising to loom over her. A single word left him. A command. "More." He'd never *felt* more beastly.

Splayed beneath him, she smiled with something akin to tenderness.

This. This was how he liked her best, he decided. Pinned by his strength. His willing captive. He could do anything…

Instinct took over. He touched her everywhere *except* the places she expected. He mapped the shells of her ears. Along her jawline. The entire length of her collarbone. A caress of each finger, even the spaces between them. Up both arms, lingering in the dips of her elbows.

Goosebumps sprang up as he manipulated the fabric of her gown and explored her belly. Her navel fascinated him. And her legs! He swallowed a groan. The backs of her knees... Was there anything softer? Oh, the sounds she made. Gasps and moans. Breathy sighs.

"You're driving me mad," she murmured. How shocked she appeared. How flushed and wonderfully needy.

What a heady thought. "I'm having fun, as you advised." Enjoying himself for the first time in...ever.

She shivered beneath him. "Don't you want to do more?"

"And rush this?" Had no one else taken the time to learn every nuance of her? Unless... He froze. "Do you wish me to hurry?"

"No!" she burst out, and his strain evaporated. "I'd be happy if you *never* stopped."

Truly? Emboldened, Brochan uttered what he hoped was a dejected sigh. "All this chatter has made me forget where I was. Now I must start over."

She gaped at him. "Start over? Like, from the beginning?"

Her next whimper drew the beginning of a smile to his lips. And yes, he absolutely started over, caressing her face, collar, arms, fingers, legs, belly. Her tremors never ceased. Nor did his.

When he could take no more of the sweet torture, he bent his head, claiming her lips, soon dizzy with need. He yanked the top of her dress. *Careful, careful.* With kisses and nips, he descended the length of her vulnerable throat and played with another part of her...

"Brochan!" She scraped her nails through his hair.

The urge to behold her expression too powerful to ignore, he lifted his head. Jolt! *She likes this. Likes* me. Her eyes were closed, her red lips puffy and parted.

Her eyelids cracked open; her whiskey eyes glazed. "More, Brochan."

"Yes. More." Never had he experienced anything like this. Never had he experienced anything like *her*.

Growling, he flared his wings and propelled himself to his knees. Determination injected straight into his muscles, his bones. Woe to anyone who tried to take this female from him.

* * * *

Viola trembled as Brochan examined her, no doubt studying the effects of his touch on her body. His features were tight, his horns flared and as straight as a ruler. His eyes glittered, his pupils eclipsing his irises. Only a rim of silver remained. Every breath caused his chest to heave.

He'd taken control, making her ache beyond reason. She *needed*…him. Just him.

"If you were mine, you would lack nothing. I would make sure of it." His gravelly tone contained a note of possession.

"Do you want me to be yours?" *I might agree.*

He inhaled a deep breath, as if preparing for what lay ahead. Then… Rather than responding, he reached out with a trembling hand. Gaze transfixed, he stroked between her legs.

"Yes!" She arched into his touch.

"You're aroused." His jaw slackened, and he flipped his attention to her face. "For me."

Shivers of exhilaration coursed through her. "You promised me more, Brochan," she said, wondering if she sounded drunk to him.

"Is this what you seek, goddess?" He sank a finger deep into her core.

"Yes!" she cried. "That!"

In, out. "Will any lover do?"

Someone certainly loved the sensual power he wielded. Good thing she loved it too. "Only you. You make me feel *so good*." She trembled with every inward glide. "Don't you dare stop."

"I'd rather die again." He bared his teeth at her. "Did you think of me while I was gone, goddess?" Thrust in. Out. "Did you dream of me?"

She knew what he wanted to hear…knew he sought a confession…knew she shouldn't…she…argh! *Can't think.* "*Yes!*"

"I thought of you too, and I'm going to do everything I imagined." In. Out. "You're going to scream and beg."

Beg? Viola? No! Absolutely not. But…maybe? "Tell me what you imagined," she commanded between rasping breaths. "And I might *allow* you to do them…"

Would he beg for *her?*

"Allow me?" He chuckled—and added a second finger. "You are mere minutes away from the satisfaction you seek. You'll let me do anything I desire."

He wasn't wrong. Her head spun. Even as concerns rose, they burned to ash. Pressure mounted, pleasure threatening to sharpen into pain. She thrashed, lost in the throes.

"Say it," he demanded.

"Yes, yes! Anything."

"And what if I *do* stop touching you, hmm?" His white-hot gaze worked in tandem with his fingers. He was a male on the cusp of bliss and agony, totally focused on her. "Will you beg me *then?*"

"I...I'll finish myself?" A question when it should have been a statement. *Could* she finish herself? Her body yearned for his wild need and his reverent caresses.

Another hiss. "Understand me, goddess. You will not take what belongs to me. Not ever again."

Her climax belonged to him? *Why do I love this so much?* She arched into his touch, gasping, "How about this? Stop, and I won't finish *you.*"

"This isn't about me," he growled, his frustration a sudden, frantic pulse against her skin.

Wait. He planned to deny himself? To hide the ferocity of his need for her? Oh, no, no, no.

Though nearly mindless, she linked an arm around his neck, holding his face mere inches from her. With her free hand, she tore at his fly. He went predator-still. Sunlight bathed him, his blue skin glinting. His incredible scent filled her head, her lungs, branding her as surely as his touch.

Their gazes met. She gripped the base of his length.

He sucked in a breath. "What are you doing, Viola?"

"Finishing you. Be a good captor and let me?"

Strain etched every line of his magnificent face, fury and desire warring in his eyes. His inhalations shallowed, but still he shook his head. "Only you."

He denies me? Eyes narrowing, she clutched the upper part of his wing with her free hand. Her claws curled against the rigid arch, ensuring the captive became the captor. Then...

She stroked him.

Just like that, his resistance frayed. With a snarl, he wrenched down and kissed her. Harder than before. Faster. Victory had never been sweeter. He branded her—owned her. Like a living flame, she burned for him.

Reaching between them, he clasped her wrist. He squeezed until she released her prize, then raised and pinned her arm over her head. Heartbeat. Heartbeat. Appearing strained, he removed his hand from her core.

A protest died on her tongue when he ground against her. Flesh to flesh. Male to female without penetration. She gasped.

And that was only the beginning.

He mimicked the motions of sex, grinding, thrusting, driving her into madness.

The kiss stretched on and on. They devoured each other, exchanging breath and passion. All the while, he caressed her with his free hand, his touch remaining gentle. The juxtaposition only maddened her further, pressure and pleasure coiling together, threatening to shatter.

Broken gasps bled into ragged moans. So good, so good, so good. *Want him.*

Need him.

Too much? Never had she craved like this, roiling inside. All because of a warrior who desired her but didn't like her.

Qualms reignited, but she was too far gone to care. "Brochan. I...you...we..."

With ruthless precision, he worked himself against her. As they both shuddered with need, steam curled from their bodies, filling the little space between them until...

The pressure broke.

Viola hurled over the edge with a scream at the same time he threw back his head and roared. They clung to each other, lost...

But finally found?

Chapter Nine

Elation and shame beat through Brochan. He'd made a goddess climax. He'd made *Viola* climax, the most complicated goddess of all. He'd reveled in her cries of abandon and feared he might never be the same.

He'd done it. He'd succumbed to temptation at long last, taking what his brother was soon to die for—this woman's every touch.

He was a terrible sibling, and a worse father. He deserved a severe beating. What's more, he'd taken what Viola wouldn't have given him if other males had been present.

As she stirred beneath him, unveiling a satisfied smile, his chest clenched. His shame magnified when he spied streaks of white on her dress. And yet, already he hungered for her anew.

Though he crumbled on the inside, he hardened on the outside. How did she do this to him?

He whipped off his shirt, only then realizing he'd left it on, forgoing the pleasure of skin-to-skin contact. A mistake he wouldn't make again. Or ever. Because he would *not* touch her a second time. Definitely not a third.

Tongue glued to the roof of his mouth, he wiped her dress before standing. He looked anywhere but at the goddess as he zipped up. "Fix your clothing." *Please.* Before his mind short-circuited.

Sounding both sad and angry, she said, "You're going to make me regret what happened here, aren't you?" She eased into a seated position. "Well, no need to scold me for being so wanton with you. Narcissism has decided to punish me on your behalf."

Confusion struck. What did she mean? Punish her? Punish her how?

And why? She'd gotten everything she'd wanted—his total surrender.

Scowling, he reached out to offer her a hand. "We should head back to the palace."

"Oh yes, you're going to make me regret what happened," she muttered, standing under her own steam.

He gave her dress time to fall into place before facing her.

The first thing he noticed? The flicker of pain flashing in her whiskey eyes. Then her lips parted, a moan slipping free. The color draining from her cheeks. Rubbing her temples, she lamented, "Not here. Not now."

Her knees gave out, and she collapsed.

Brochan flapped his wings, catching her before she hit the ground. "What's wrong?" Merely a trick? Or had he harmed her somehow? He swept her against his chest.

"They're rising. All of them. Flooding me." She pulled at hanks of her hair. "Make them stop!"

Concern swamped him. "Tell me what's wrong, Viola. Now!" Before he razed the realm.

"Don't you see? I'm unlovable," she cried, sobbing. Anguished. "I'm so ugly inside. So so so so so so so so ugly. You should kill me, Brochan. Yes! Kill me." Desperate, she sank her little claws into his pectorals, peering up at him through heartbreaking eyes. Tears poured down her cheeks. "I don't deserve to live for what I did to McCadden. You want to do the deed, and you should. *Please.*"

Razors slashed at his insides. What was even happening right now? His mind could not process this. "Viola?"

"I'm as horrid as the demon. Worthy only of suffering. I promise I won't fight you when you strike. Okay? All right? Just…swear you'll make it hurt. For the sake of justice, I should perish screaming." New sobs bubbled from her. "Please, Brochan. The truth has never been so clear."

How earnest she appeared. How broken she sounded. Something cracked inside his chest, acid leaking out, spilling into his veins. He'd followed this female for months, yet he'd never witnessed anything like this, every ounce of her confidence stripped away. The demon—

Comprehension dawned, and he narrowed his eyes. The demon. *Narcissism did this—with my help.* The punishment she'd mentioned.

Great adoration equaled great self-love. Great disdain after great adoration meant greater self-hatred. No wonder she sought to prevent this, whatever lines she must cross. Who could endure it?

The acid scorched layer upon layer of his fury, leaving only raw instinct. He acted without thought. Nuzzling his scruffy cheek against her damp one, he said, "I think you are the most beautiful creature I've ever beheld. I have craved you since the moment I first spied you."

She went still. "You have?" Her nose wrinkled, her brows drawing together. She opened and closed her mouth as if not sure how to reply.

Different emotions flared in her incredible eyes. Misery gave way to surprise, then uncertainty, which gradually dulled, revealing assurance.

"Brochan, that's just so...*shallow* of you. I, at least, notice a person's *intelligence* first." She canted her head, pensive. "Although, I suppose I'll have to forgive you. Because I have such a gracious heart and all. The most gracious!"

Relief poured through him, and he gripped her tighter. Gut-wrenching tension eased. Her confidence had returned, and he prayed it never faded again.

He had some thinking to do, he realized. Some new decisions to make.

"Oh, goodness." With a tinkling laugh, she dabbed at her rosy skin. "I'm so glad I'm a pretty crier."

"The prettiest," they said in unison, and she lifted her chin higher.

"Let's return to your story about first spying me." She settled comfortably into the cradle of his arms, nestling against him. "Tell me every thought you entertained about my every feature. Start with my silken hair and hypnotizing eyes. Leave nothing out."

"I will not." He jumped and flapped his wings, catching a current of air. They soared through the sky, heading toward the plethora of suns currently setting in the distance.

"I promise not to laugh at you more than a little."

"Now you try my patience."

Locks of pale hair whipped over his face as she snuggled closer. "You're so obsessed with me. On a scale of one to ten, you rate me a twelve."

"And you rate me a zero."

"Hardly. I give you at least two points for your good taste in goddesses."

He pursed his lips. "I was in the bar the day you met McCadden. You walked right past me."

"Did you have these horns back then?" She made a playful scratching motion. "Because meow."

Had he been walking rather than flying, he might have stumbled; her words knocked him for a loop. "You like my horns?" After a reluctant pause, he added, "They aren't too beastly?"

Leering at him, she licked her upper lip. "They're just the right amount."

His heart stuttered, his body once again at war with his mind. He fought the surge of desire to the best of his ability, resolved to resist her—for now. First he needed to digest everything he'd learned about this woman. He must determine whether she'd spoken true or lied about McCadden's near-death, and how he felt about it, whatever the answer. At the very least, Viola wasn't the merciless seductress he'd once considered her. Mostly, he should figure out how to proceed with her. Did he owe her any kind of punishment? Thanks? He didn't know anything anymore.

The palace appeared on the horizon. He propelled his mind in a different direction. "Now that we've called a temporary truce and agreed to a partnership, we should devise our plan of attack against the other Forsaken."

"No worries. I've already worked up the perfect scheme. I considered doing it to you when you cuffed me at the beach." She petted his chest. "Check it. I'm the goddess of the Afterlife, right? I'm able to remove more than a lifeforce. I can reach inside anyone and pluck out their spiritual heart, the *container* of the lifeforce. Neither a body nor a spirit can exist without it. I'll be honest, though. I've never tried it on a deathless being, because I've never *faced* a deathless being."

He blinked at her creativity. Knowing she could have attempted this on him but hadn't... *She truly isn't the monster I thought her to be.* He had much more to consider than he'd realized.

"We'll try it," he said, surprising himself. He—A shadow shifted inside the palace, near a window in the throne room.

Someone moved about inside? One of the Forsaken? Did others lurk throughout the palace, waiting for an opportunity to strike? Fury sparked.

"We have company," he informed Viola. "When I flash you on the balcony, stay there. Do you understand? Hide in a corner until I return to collect you."

"You're planning an attack? While I'm wearing my cuff?" Panicked, she wiggled and scrambled until she was able to wrap her legs around his waist and put her face directly in front of his. "The invader might not mean us any harm. Or you're mistaken about seeing someone. Or any other excuse you'll believe. Let's take a moment to investigate before we strike at someone we shouldn't strike at. Okay?"

Why act this way? Did she know something he didn't? Suspicions prodded him. Closing in… "Do as I command, goddess."

"Listen to me," she said, her panic intensifying. "If there's danger, you need to remove my cuff. If there's no danger, you could inadvertently attack your closest friends."

"I have no friends."

"You wouldn't want to accidentally harm an innocent, would you?" She clasped his chin, doing her best to catch his gaze as he angled his body, preparing to flash. "Brochan—"

He flashed to the balcony.

"I demand you stay with me!" She sank her claws into his shoulders, ensuring he could not detangle from her. Hysteria and rage contorted her features.

Determined to protect her and not knowing what else to do, he *forced* a separation. Before she could latch on again, he dove, flashing through the doors, solidifying inside the throne room. His momentum continued from one side to the other, aggression charging him as he slammed into—

Shock inundated Brochan when the man's identity clicked. He and McCadden tumbled across the floor, stopping at Farrow's feet.

The visitors hadn't changed clothes since the battle, both wearing garments splattered in the blood of the Forsaken. The only difference? Soot now smeared them.

"My apologies." Brochan flapped his wings, rising and pulling his brother to his feet. Guilt engulfed him as he recalled what he'd been doing less than half an hour ago. "How did you find me? Has something else occurred?" Another attack?

Before his brother or Farrow had a chance to respond, Viola catapulted into the room. His eyes widened. She'd shifted into her other form. A *kitten*. He'd seen her shift only once, but it had happened at a distance. Someone had threatened her pet, and that someone had died screaming, shredded by her claws. Up close, Brochan picked up astonishing details he'd missed.

She still wore her dress. And she was utterly adorable. A pair of tiny horns resembled cat ears. Patches of red-orange fur made her appear both soft and scaled. Crimson eyes glowed, her pupils nothing but thin slits. Fangs extended over her bottom lip.

Why did she shift like this? Other demon-hosting immortals did not.

Focus. With her murder mittens bared, she flew closer. McCadden and Farrow geared to defend. Brochan flared his wings, knocking the pair backward and catching Viola against his chest.

"No one touches her!" he grated as he struggled to contain her.

They grappled for supremacy. She was a bundle of fury, and she showed no mercy, attacking to maim. Or worse. Anger sparked, but it was dulled by incredulity. All this because he left her safely on a balcony?

He landed no blows. Even now, he couldn't bring himself to injure her. Twice he caught his brother's shocked gaze.

"Stop this, kitten. Before you injure yourself." Brochan's gentle tone surprised even him.

"You do *not* hurt my baby!" she screeched.

His gaze zoomed back to his brother, whose jaw dropped.

The goddess fought for the devil-dog? He glared as he dodged a particularly nasty blow to his testicles. Viola took advantage of the opportunity and shredded his upper body. Blood poured.

"I haven't hurt your baby," he grated. Yet.

"That's right, and you won't!" Slashing and biting, too wily to contain, she attacked with more fervor. Until she tired herself out, her movements slowing. When she noticed their audience, she finally halted. "McCadden. Strange woman I've never met. You're not Fluffy."

In a blink, Viola shifted back to her usual form and smoothed the fabric of her gown. "You must be parched," she said oh, so casually. "Shall I send Brochan to fetch us drinks?"

McCadden glowered at her, the teardrops tattooed on his face starker than usual. His pink hair shagged. The silver piercings that lined one of his eyebrows glinted in the light. His inked hands curled into hard balls of rage as he stepped toward the goddess.

Brochan enfolded Viola in his wings and drew her against his chest. Hands flat on his pectorals, she blinked up at him, panting.

"Do you want to explain what just happened?" Though he'd already guessed the answer. She'd expected her pet to be here. Likely the reason for her earlier burst of joy.

"No, thank you," she said, turning to face their audience. "In case you didn't notice, we have guests."

He slung an arm around her waist, locking her in place lest she dart off. But she didn't attempt to run or fight. No, she pressed against him. Without thought, he zoomed his gaze to his brother once more. Still glowering. Heat suffused Brochan's cheeks, a slight tinge of guilt flaring, but he did not adjust his stance.

"Hello, and welcome to our starter palace," Viola said, suddenly full of cheer. "Please ignore the construction we haven't started. A good goldsmith with reasonable rates is so hard to find these days, wouldn't you agree? Oh, that reminds me. Brochan, I meant to tell you I've decided to redecorate the entire realm. Picture it. The best kingdom anyone anywhere has ever ruled." As she spoke, she spread her arms to encompass the room, as if she were describing every minute change in elaborate detail.

Had there ever been a more fascinating creature? "How did you find me?" he inquired of Farrow. He and Viola would chat later. He would insist on it.

"Your tattoo," the Forsaken said, pointing to his arm. "I saw the coordinates before you flashed."

She'd used his own tracker against him? Why? Never mind. As if he didn't know. A possible key to Nevaeh could turn friends into enemies. "Why did you bring McCadden?"

"I was worried about you," his brother snapped. "Rightly so. The goddess clearly seeks to doom you."

Viola flinched ever so slightly. "I'm Brochan's partner. Granted, I've done the brunt of the work so far, coming up with the plan and tidying up headquarters, but I have high hopes he'll come through for us in the end."

That flinch… Brochan grazed his claws up and down her belly as if to soothe a hurt. Thankfully, his wings hid the action.

Farrow tilted her head, her attention laser-focused on Viola. "*You* are the one causing so much trouble among the Forsaken?" Her mouth curled with disdain. Death flickered in her irises, whirling, attempting to hypnotize the goddess. "Give me what I want, or I will—"

"*I said no one touches her,*" Brochan roared, clasping his prize tighter.

The other Forsaken blinked, her brow furrowing with confusion. "You guard the hider of a key?"

"He does. Savagely." Viola evinced all kinds of smugness.

A corner of his mouth twitched. He did like her confidence.

McCadden moved his gaze between Brochan and Viola, his countenance darkening.

Just like that, Brochan's amusement dissolved. Guilt became an acid rain inside him. Though his feelings toward the goddess had softened, his plans for her unclear, he knew he had no right to enjoy the female his brother had loved.

"Remain here," he said. "I will return shortly."

He flashed Viola to the master suite, where he spied an unexpected sight. Her pet was indeed here, bouncing on the bed like an unrestrained child. When the little creature spotted him, it froze before lowering into attack position and baring its fangs.

Brochan popped his jaw. "How?" he demanded.

She cringed and slunk away from him, moving between him and the creature. "You're not going to hurt him. Promise me."

He thought back. Every time she and the devil-dog had flashed together, she'd held the thing in her arms. The times she'd left it behind, it had remained behind…at least while Brochan had trailed the goddess. But what of the times in between?

Knowing he'd get no answers from her until she had his assurance, he said, "I'm not going to hurt him. Not *today*." Brochan might have softened toward the goddess, but not the devil-dog. Good men had died for the mutt.

Her eyes narrowed. "That's not good enough." She hurried over to act as the animal's shield.

"How?" he repeated. "Animals, no matter how bright, cannot flash."

"Would you believe he was in the neighborhood and stopped by to borrow a cup of sugar?"

"How?" he insisted.

"You don't deserve to know!"

"You will tell me anyway!"

She gave him a chiding look. "Must you shout? Really, Brochan. We have guests." As if she were the last sane being in the universe, she threw herself onto the bed, landing next to her pet and bouncing. The two hmphed at him before snuggling. "Speaking of the uninvited, you owe me an apology for the insult you dished me. Also, who is the female and why is she here? I distinctly remember not inviting her for tea."

He messaged the back of his neck. "Her name is Farrow, and she's a Forsaken, like me. We plan to enter Nevaeh together."

Viola jolted into an upright position, her spine ramrod straight. "Enter Nevaeh. Together, you say?" Her quiet tone set his nerves on edge.

"How did I insult you earlier?" he demanded with a jerky wave of his arms.

Another hmph. "As if you don't know."

He truly didn't. "Explain it to me."

"I'm your partner, in case you've forgotten. You're supposed to confirm absolutely everything I say."

She could not be serious.

"Really, Brochan, if you can't be a good ally to others, don't expect us to be a good ally to you." She followed her snotty tone with kissy noises at her pet. "So? Is my baby safe forever or not?"

Frustrating female! "I won't harm it, but I won't help it either." The admission burned Brochan's tongue.

She reacted as if he'd struck her. "It?"

"Female—"

"No. Not another word from you." Viola extended her arm in expectation. The cuff gleamed on her wrist. "The time for action has come. Kindly remove this hideous piece of hardware. It clashes with my free will."

He held on to his stubbornness. "Give me the key, and I'll remove the cuff."

"Remove the cuff, and I'll give you a key."

He...couldn't. No, he wouldn't. Maybe she wasn't a wicked temptress who lied and charmed and worked her wiles on unsuspecting men. But maybe she was. If he removed the cuff, and she flashed, forcing him to chase her...no. He wouldn't risk dividing his attention between his brother and his woman—er, his partner. Not until he'd thought things through. "Just...stay here with your devil-dog while I deal with the guests. We'll discuss the cuff tomorrow."

Chapter Ten

"We'll discuss the cuff tomorrow," Viola muttered as she stormed across the palace grounds. A lush garden had come alive almost overnight, just like the oasis. Grass, trees and a multitude of flowers had sprouted below her bedroom balcony. Insects and a few small animals had shown up too. They must have been here all along, seemingly as dead as everything else.

For the first time, those insects and animals darted from her. Sensed the danger of her temper, did they?

Days had passed since the arrival of McCadden and Farrow, but Viola and Brochan hadn't discussed *anything*. Not even their rainy interlude, when he'd shocked and thrilled her with his reverent exploration of her body. Or the fact that he'd called her "kitten," a nickname that had made her heart flutter.

Viola's patience had worn thin. Did he not realize how important she was to him? To the entire realm? How important it was to keep her happy? This incomparable, bloom-scented air would fade with a single command from her. The world sought to please *her*. Where was her thanks? Her appreciation?

Something needed to be done. Soon. Unfortunately for Brochan, there was no better doer than Viola. They would be reopening the discussion about the cuff *today*. Along with the Forsaken they planned to kill and the fact that Brochan hadn't adored her for an hour a day, as agreed.

She whirled around and raced toward the palace, more than ready to confront him.

He's embarrassed by his attraction to you and hopes to keep your arrangement a secret.

Her step slowed, tremors nearly buckling her knees. Was Narcissism correct? Did Brochan wish to keep their arrangement—and his growing affection for her—a secret?

Acid leaked through her chest, her eyes stinging. Stinging? With tears? Anger replaced sorrow. How dare he?! Brochan should be *proud* of her. If she could date herself, she would. There was a good chance she was her own fated mate!

Inhale. Exhale. Okay. All right. A measure of calm settled over her. Whatever his feelings about her, he still desired her. That wasn't in question. While they hadn't spoken and he'd avoided her as much as possible, they *had* interacted a time or two. His smoldering gaze had kept her strong. A first for her.

Viola quickened her step as soon as she entered the palace. Oof! She bounced into someone. McCadden, she realized with disappointment. As soon as she caught herself, she noticed the moderately attractive Farrow poised behind him.

Point number four on Viola's list of grievances. If McCadden occupied a chamber and she entered, he immediately stomped out. He spoke to her only in passing, and only to issue insults. Well, no more.

Today, he would hear her out, just like his brother, and that was that. She'd made a mistake with him, and she was big enough to admit it. A tiny mistake, yes, but a mistake all the same. And perhaps she could have maybe, possibly treated him a wee bit better after she'd gotten what she wanted from him instead of taking his gift, taunting him and fleeing.

"McCadden," she began. "I'm glad you were rude enough to be in my way. I've wished to speak with you and apol—"

"Cease speaking." His lip curled. He backed her against the wall and snarled, "Stay away from my brother." Clearly not ready to listen or forgive, he stomped off before she could respond.

Strike one. Her shoulders slumped, until she rebounded. What were the odds of a second failure in one day? Zero point zero. Viola never crashed twice.

Farrow remained in place, watching her with an intense, unwavering stare.

How irritating! "I only wished to tell him I was sorry," she informed the other woman.

"I wonder how lovely you'll consider yourself when I carve you into pieces."

She fluffed her hair. "Wonder no more. I'll love it. The more pieces of me the better."

If the woman hadn't been taking up so much of Brochan's attention, Viola might have liked her. But the two Forsaken were almost always together, whispering and planning their future in the skies. Jealousy seethed inside of her every time she glimpsed them together.

"I'll take your head. Soon. The day is coming." The other woman strutted off, following McCadden.

"If you want a girls' night, just say so," she called. *Strike two.* Perhaps she should avoid Brochan, just in case this bad luck continued.

No! But now more than ever, the cuff had to go. Trying to fight Brochan, McCadden and Farrow without full use of her abilities... She shuddered. If one or all the trio attacked her, she must be prepared. Strong.

The meeting with Brochan could wait a few minutes, though. First, she would outfit herself appropriately.

She rushed to the master suite and selected a scarlet gown. The sheer material revealed more than it concealed. As requested, Fluffy had collected her go-bag, ensuring she donned the perfect jewelry. A necklace with dangling bullets. A gun ring that utilized those bullets. Another ring with a minuscule saw hidden beneath the center stone. Another winding bracelet, able to elongate and lock into place, becoming a sword. Each piece had been crafted from a different kind of metal to combat different kinds of creatures.

Confidence restored, Viola marched through the palace she'd been cleaning bit by bit. This time, Fluffy kept pace at her side, his little trot as adorable as ever. "I'll find Brochan and grant him an opportunity to fix his errors," she explained. She missed their easy camaraderie in the oasis. Missed getting to know him and letting him get to know her. No one's glance affected her like his. His compliments were an aphrodisiac.

Her child twittered. Translation: *Brilliant plan, Momma.*

"Trust me, baby. I know."

If Brochan opted not to remove the cuff, Viola would have no choice but to wash her hands of him, ending their partnership for good. She refused to live in a cage. And she most assuredly refused to be relegated to the sidelines. One of the reasons she'd left Cameo and the other Lords of the Underworld. Other demon-oppressed immortals she considered friends. They adored her, like everyone else, but they didn't value her battle skill.

Maybe she was a fool to team up with a beast who built her up one moment and tore her down the next—the same MO as the demon. Not to mention his hatred for her beloved fur-child. Brochan still scowled and cursed whenever he caught sight of Fluffy.

Viola flattened a hand over her churning stomach. Upon her escape from her mother's gilded cage, she'd been unprepared for the rest of the world. She'd fallen for the first boy to smile at her, easily parted with her virginity, and woke up alone and forgotten. Used. The pattern had continued, eroding an already fragile sense of self-worth.

She'd been a shell of her former self when she'd found Fluffy, injured and abandoned by his kind. She'd doctored and raised him. Again and again, he'd proven his loyalty to her, risking his life to save hers. How dare Brochan think *his* loved one mattered more than hers?

Voices carried from the throne room, and she picked up speed, gliding through the open double doors.

The trio stood around a table positioned in the center of the room, the top littered with scrolls and maps. Her churning worsened. Once again, the group had opted to exclude her.

"—ambush here, here and here in unison," Brochan was saying, tapping a claw on different locations of a map. As if he sensed her presence, he flipped up his gaze. His jaw went slack, his horns standing straight up. A sign of excitement. Or maybe aggression. Those silvery irises blazed, sending shivers down her spine.

"Who do you plan to ambush?" she asked.

"Farrow spied one of the warriors we burned." He looked her over and gulped. "They live on."

Narcissism attempted to speak, but her delight drowned out the fiend's voice.

Her ferocious male towered so tall and proud, wearing a plain white T-shirt and black leathers. The perfect complement to his lovely cerulean skin. His dark hair stood on end, and his wings rippled with hostility. Why had she never taken the time to caress every inch of them?

A mystery to solve later. *Let's do this.*

Gliding forward, she pasted on a smile. "Thank you so very much for assembling and awaiting my arrival."

McCadden bristled, and Farrow stiffened. Probably with envy. No one commanded a room better than Viola.

Brochan white-knuckled the table while tracking her every move. "Do you need something, goddess?"

"Many things. All of which are owed to me. Shall I remind you of our bargain, beast? I'm happy to explain the minute details to our guests, if you'd like, but one way or another, the conversation is taking place *now*."

A muscle jumped under his eye before he nodded. "Leave us," he said to McCadden and Farrow.

The Fallen One protested but obeyed, while the Forsaken glowered and flashed away.

Brochan moved to a backless chair at the foot of the table and eased down as if he carried a heavy weight and needed relief. "Talk."

She bent to pet Fluffy's precious head and kiss his little snout. "Return to the bedroom, darling. If Brochan is a good boy, Mommy will reward him greatly."

Eyes glittering with disgust, he vanished in a hurry.

Brochan sat up straighter. "Why did you name him Fluffy?"

As if he cared. No doubt he merely stalled. Even still, she told him, "The years I spent locked inside my mother's secret home, I read to occupy my time," she explained as she straightened. "My favorite story revolved around a magical teddy bear named Princess Fluffikans."

Brochan flinched and rubbed the spot over his heart.

Interesting reaction. Swishing her hips, Viola closed the rest of the distance, swept a pile of papers to the floor, and hopped onto the table directly in front of him.

"Let me guess. You're here for the removal of the cuff," he said, a hitch in his voice.

"Among other things."

"You also expect me to adore you."

"I do, yes." Bracing her arms behind her, she reclined at a slight angle. The slits in her skirt allowed her to place one foot on each arm of his chair. "But only because you do, in fact, adore me."

He wrapped his hands around her ankles with a stronger grip than she'd expected. Tremors migrated from him to her. "I...might," he admitted.

A shock strong enough to wrench the truth from her. "I desire a real chance with you. I like being with you. I like *you*. And I suspect I'll *really* like being with you when I'm here of my own volition. Wouldn't you like that? Knowing I'm here because I want to be, not because I'm compelled?"

He closed his eyes for a moment, his long lashes casting spiky shadows over his cheeks. He breathed deeply, his body emitting great waves of strain.

Hope surged. She pressed her advantage. "In return for the cuff's removal, I have a marvelous idea to ensure McCadden's immortality. It's not a trip to Nevaeh, but it does buy your brother some time."

His brows dropped low over his eyes. "Why won't you give me the key?"

"Hand it over so you can shack up with another woman?" She scoffed. "Don't be such a child."

His jaw went slack. "You're...jealous of Farrow?"

Her? Jealous? She sucked air between her teeth. "How dare you? Do you even know how ridiculous you sound? Why, I've never been jealous of anyone or anything a single second of my life. I'm far too perfect!"

"You are. You're jealous." Tendrils of satisfaction and delight wafted from him. Perhaps even a twinge of wonder. "Let me take McCadden past the veil, and I'll return the key to you. I'll adore every inch of you again."

Her heart leaped. *Careful.* "What if I...lost the key? Or something."

He stiffened, his satisfaction, delight and wonder dying a swift death. "Did you?"

"I...you...it doesn't matter! Not until you remove the cuff. As soon as you do, I'll adore every inch of *you.*"

The muscle beneath his eye jumped again. "My answer is...no."

He'd hesitated. She was making progress! "I think your measuring stick is disagreeing with you again."

"It is," he hissed, only to jut his chin.

"Remove the cuff. I'll make you so glad you did."

"I...no." His voice hardened. "I don't trust you enough. And I don't wish to hurt McCadden any more than necessary. I raised him, Viola. He's my brother, yes, but he's also my son. He's felt worthless most of his life, and his experience with you didn't help that. For me to choose you over him, even temporarily...I can't do that to him."

The demon swooped in, whispering her deepest fears. *Unlovable. Unwanted. Forsaken.* Just as Brochan had once proclaimed.

Her shoulders rolled in even as she fought to maintain a cordial expression. Another strike. Her bottom lip trembled.

Brochan rubbed the tattoo on his arm and frowned. "Viola—"

"Not another word from you. I'm thinking." Or rather, masking her reaction. She reclined fully, lying flat and peering up at the vaulted ceiling. She would give this male one more chance. Just one more. She'd come too far with him to stop now. Besides, secret parts of her *longed* for his unconditional acceptance. The same way she'd once longed for her mother's unconditional love.

Why did she always pick the hopeless cases?

No, no. Not hopeless. Not yet. "Let me verify I understand you correctly," she said. "Your brother hates me, so you won't touch me. You make him feel worthy by making me feel unworthy. Yes?"

He stiffened, released her, and scrubbed a hand over his tired features. "Haven't you done the same to countless others?"

"Haven't you learned from my mistakes?" she snipped, blinking away tears. Two could play the blame game.

A growl rumbled from him. "I'll never pass your test, Viola."

"We can't know until I actually test you. But I can't test you until you admit your great love for me." Bitterness seeped into her tone. "Besides, I'm not offering forever right now. Only a limited-time, too-good-to-miss opportunity to spend more time with me."

"Time, yes," he rushed out with an eager nod. "Just give me more time. You wear the cuff while I figure this out. So much has changed. I must unravel the particulars before I act."

"You misunderstand." Once her tears had dried, she eased to her feet. "Remove the cuff, or I'm done with you."

His tortured gaze searched hers, and he repeated, "Just give me more time, kitten."

Kitten now. Her favorite endearment paired with a final denial. Things began to shatter inside Viola. Scabs sloughed off internal wounds, leaving them raw and oozing. Strength drained, and her limbs quaked.

Even still, she smiled brightly. As she used to smile for her mother. "Of course. More time." She patted his cheek. "Take all the time you need. Now, if you'll excuse me, I must check on Fluffy. We wouldn't want him to pee all over your shoes in the closet, would we? Not again."

Brochan clutched the arms of his chair again as if to stop himself from reaching for her. "Viola. Goddess."

"No. Nothing more needs to be said. Goodbye, Brochan." She strolled from the throne room as if she hadn't a care.

He didn't call her back.

McCadden waited just outside the doors, his body vibrating with fury. Had he listened in? He stared at her as she passed him, silent.

Somehow, she maintained her casual façade all the way to the bedroom, where Fluffy played his two favorite games in unison: Zoomies and the Floor is Lava, bouncing from one piece of furniture to another at breathtaking speed.

She shut and locked the door, even knowing Brochan had only to flash to enter. Her pet sensed her distress and leaped into her arms to nuzzle and comfort her. "We're blowing this joint, darling." She kissed his face and set him down. "Be a dear and fetch Mommy's ax."

He raced to the duffel bag she'd hidden under the bed, then returned with a small, golden ax in his mouth. She dropped to her knees and petted his head, cooing words of praise before claiming the weapon.

A plan formed days ago. A good one. Brochan would never be able to find her.

She'd meant what she said.

This was goodbye.

Chapter Eleven

Brochan anchored his elbows on the tabletop and bowed his head, resting his brow in his upraised palms. Had he just made a grave error?

Viola had offered him everything he'd ever wanted. A chance to enjoy her at his leisure. To explore her body and soul, learning the most minute nuances of her past. Everything that made her who she was—the female who fascinated him beyond measure and drew him without cease. He wouldn't have to wonder what she wanted; she would always tell him. He could ensure she remained well complimented and brimming with satisfaction while she filled his life with excitement and awe.

Could she be happy with someone like him? Truly happy long-term?

Would she move on when he failed her test?

Indecision tore at him. How could he choose Viola over McCadden? But how could he choose McCadden over the goddess? He needed them both in his life. His brother and...his woman. A female he'd kissed and caressed only once. Not nearly enough.

How was he supposed to reconcile his conflicting desires? Especially when he already knew the outcome of her test. He would fail, just like his brother, who'd chosen Brochan over the goddess.

How could Brochan do any less? But how could he let her go?

"Brother?" McCadden cupped his shoulder, drawing him out of his mind.

Without lifting his gaze, he reached up and patted his brother's hand. While he remained in his chair, McCadden stood at his side.

Would the male forgive him if he courted the goddess, as every fiber of his being demanded?

"She is different with you than she ever was with me." There was an odd inflection in his brother's tone. McCadden eased into the chair next to Brochan's. "After our introduction, Viola never sought me out, even though she planned to use me. I had to seek her. Looking back, I realize she never uttered a kind word about me, only herself. At the time, I was too enamored of her to recognize I was the only one invested in our relationship."

"But?"

"Despite her changes, I still don't trust her."

"I know. And yet…I want her anyway," he admitted, shame coating every syllable. "I want her more than I've ever wanted anything."

"And if she's using you the way she used me?"

She might be. How could he know unless he took a chance? Except, a part of him suspected the beauty who'd experienced such a painful childhood might actually mean what she'd said—she liked him.

The pain he'd continued to glimpse inside her never failed to lance his heart. Not to mention the self-hatred she usually hid so well. He remembered the joy she'd evinced as she danced in the rain, and a groan of regret lodged in his throat.

He flipped up his gaze, meeting his brother's intense stare. "Do you seek to live forever, McCadden?" The words croaked from him.

McCadden jerked as if punched. "I—"

Searing pain suddenly erupted in Brochan's forearm, on his tattoo, and he hissed. He jolted upright with a single thought. *Viola.* He jumped to his feet. "The goddess. Something's wrong." He didn't wait for a response, just flashed to her bedroom, shouting her name.

There was no sign of her…only a pool of blood near the hearth. She'd been…she was… Horror punched him. A severed hand rested in the center of the blood—the tiny pink claws curled in with her fingers, except for the middle one, which was extended. The cuff lay next to the appendage. So did an ax.

Realization: She'd done this to herself. She'd chopped off her hand to escape him. All because he had refused to work with her. Instead, he'd worked against her. Of course, she'd left him. Anyone with good sense would have done the same.

Agony birthed a soul-deep roar. Frantic to find her, to help and protect her as she healed—she must heal—he studied his tattoo. The image showed her location was…nowhere.

The inside of his chest raw and stinging, he slapped the map. Shook his arm.

No change. He couldn't track her. Couldn't sense her.

Panic sprouted, gaining ground fast. Where had she gone? *Think, think.* He'd followed her for months. She'd visited hundreds of realms, homes and areas. But she'd frequented one place more than any other.

Hopeful, Brochan flashed to the mortal realm. Budapest, Hungary. A dark, overcast sky framed a massive stone fortress seated atop a tree-lined hill. When they weren't warring in the Underworld, a band of demon-bonded immortals and their assortment of significant others lived here. The powerful men and women bore no love for Brochan.

A cool breeze clapped branches together. Insects sang. No unusual activity outside the fortress.

Though Brochan comprehended the danger, he flashed inside the fortress. Empty rooms. Unmade beds. Haphazardly emptied closets. A half-filled coffee mug on the kitchen counter. Cold. The occupants had left in a hurry. His panic sharpened.

Where was she? Weak and injured, she was easy prey for anyone interested in her harm. And the other Forsaken were *only* interested in harming her. Red dotted Brochan's vision.

Nerves frayed beyond repair, he returned to the abandoned realm. Her bedchamber. He dropped to his knees before the pool of blood, threw back his head and unleashed his roar. The palace shook. Cracks spread over the windows. Why hadn't he freed her? For the key, as he'd tried to convince himself, or his insatiable need for her?

Did she even have a key? Sometimes he wondered.

Either way, he should have given her a chance to prove herself. If she'd decided to leave him, so what? At least he would know her true desires beyond any doubt.

"Brochan?" His brother's voice infiltrated his awareness. Spotting the blood, the male rushed closer. "What happened?"

"She left." He almost couldn't get the words out of his mouth. "She left me." *And I deserved it.*

"I'll kill her!"

Before he realized he'd moved, Brochan towered in front of his brother, his fangs bared. "You will not hurt her. Do you understand?"

McCadden blinked, nodded. "Even after this, you want her." A statement, not a question. First, he displayed shock, then astonishment.

"I'll always want her," he croaked. Why not admit the rest? "She is...mine. My female. The one meant for me alone." *My mate. My wife.*

Whatever the term, Viola was it for Brochan.

He'd merely played with the supposition before. But the truth was so clear now. How had he ever doubted it?

He turned to his brother. "I hate that you are pained by this. I don't wish to lose you over it. But I need her. If she'll have me, I will devote my life to making her happy." Words he should have spoken the moment his brother arrived. To McCadden, and to Viola. "I will find her. I must."

McCadden drew in a deep breath. He offered another nod, this one clipped. "I think you're a fool for doing this. She cares for only herself and her mutt, and she *will* hurt you at some point. But I won't stand in your way. I'll even aid in your search."

"Thank you." Brochan yanked his brother close for a quick hug, then stalked into the closet to gather his weapons. If anyone got in his way, they died. Nothing would stop him from claiming his mate.

* * * *

Viola stumbled through a forest shrouded in darkness, Fluffy keeping pace beside her. Her heart knocked against her ribs with every step. Branches and foliage sliced her. A gash on her forehead leaked, blood dripping into her eyes, but she didn't slow. Immortals hunted her.

Narcissism toyed with Viola all the while, reminding her of everyone she'd ever betrayed. *Worse than my mother.*

She tried to distract herself with a plan to save McCadden. What if she turned him into a vampire instead of sharing a piece of her heart? Unlike Fluffy, he was built for long term immortality. But. Turning wasn't as easy as books and movies claimed, but as a goddess of the Afterlife, she could ensure he survived the transformation. Of course, vamps were an abomination to Sent Ones. Even former Sent Ones. Good news was, he would live without having to feast on living batteries. Not that Viola cared about McCadden and his family. Brochan was hardly more than an afterthought.

Except he wasn't.

A sob bubbled from her, and Fluffy brushed against her leg, offering comfort. If not for her fur-baby, she might have ceased running and let the immortals catch her.

Yes. Do it. Narcissism had stopped trying to fuel any kind of false self-love and started revealing unshakable truths. The demon despised her very being, its every suggestion meant to cause misery. Hers. Others. If not now, later.

"No," Viola snapped. Her lover's attention might empower her in ways no one else's ever had, but his rejection cut worse. Besides, she *couldn't* flash, her physical weakness too great.

Since leaving him, she'd lost track of time. She thought two days had passed. Maybe a week. Or a year. So why hadn't her hand grown back?

Tears welled, a few escaping to trickle down her cheeks. Was she dependent on Brochan now? Without his adoration, she might remain in this weakened state forever. Part of her didn't *want* to heal. Did she even deserve to?

A branch tip grazed the raw, bloody stump, agonizing her, and she cried out.

Voices called from the distance.

"I heard her!"

"This way!"

"She's my kill. Get in my way and suffer!"

"Flash to safety," she commanded her baby between panting breaths. "Please! I'll recover, no matter what happens, as long as I know you're okay."

His loyalty unwavering, he refused, choosing to endure or perish by her side.

Tears fell faster. If the worst happened and they were overtaken, Fluffy would fight until the bitter end. He always did. He loved her as much as she loved him, her only balm of comfort. The only reason she wasn't curled into a ball, sobbing.

Limbs and leaves crunched under her bare feet. She'd been in such a temper, she hadn't thought to change out of her dress and don boots before axing her hand.

Her mutilated wrist throbbed as she snaked around a large tree trunk. Thick buttress roots tripped her, and she tumbled down. As she crash-landed, dirt flung over the cloth that covered her wound. Nausea rose. Viola vomited the meager contents of her stomach before lumbering to her feet with Fluffy's help and forcing herself onward.

She wheezed shallow breaths, every inhalation acting as a blade to her lungs. Knowing she could go no farther, Viola dropped. She leaned against a barbed tree trunk. The sharp tips stabbed her back, adding to her collection of injuries, but she didn't care. Her vision wavered. Her head swam.

Blood rushed inside her ears, the ring deafening. "I'm so sorry, darling. Mommy needs to rest a bit. She can't...she..." A sob bubbled from her at last. She had failed her child. She had failed herself. What proved the most disheartening, however? Brochan wasn't going to rush to the rescue. Not this time.

Not that she needed to be rescued. She wasn't some goddess in distress, even when she was in distress. But she'd tasted the wonders of having a partner. Now, she was addicted.

Did he miss her at all?

A bitter laugh escaped her. Of course, he did. He wanted the key that she didn't possess.

Three males—two vampires and a berserker—exploded from a wall of foliage, stopping when they spotted her. The vampires smiled, flashing their fangs. She recognized them. Kinsman of someone she'd doomed.

The berserker evinced glee. The last time she was here, he'd hit on her, and she had rebuffed him.

Fluffy's hackles lifted, a pungent odor filling the air. His greatest defense. Few could withstand the stinging aroma. He bared his sharp little teeth and screeched so loudly while spinning in circles.

The immortals cringed and stepped back. But they didn't flee.

The taller vampire rubbed pale hands together. "Look at the high and mighty goddess now. Dressed in rags and covered in filth. Finally, the outside matches the inside."

Viola flinched. Someone lifted a sword, the metal gleaming in the moonlight. Rallying what little strength she had left, she climbed to her feet. Standing between her baby and her enemies. Or teetering between her baby and her enemies.

"Hello, gentlemen," she said with as much nonchalance as she could muster. "I'm so glad you found me. Are you here for the forgiveness seminar, too? Let's attend together. I hear there's a banquet afterward."

"I will enjoy shredding your body into too many pieces to count." The berserker's voice dripped with relish.

"You can have her body," the second vampire said, "but only after we've drained it."

"Fluffy," she intoned, and he knew her well enough to guess her expectation.

He leaped into her arms as the trio lunged for her—just as she'd hoped. At the last possible moment, Viola used what remained of her strength to mist herself and her trembling pet, becoming intangible. The men hit the trunk and stumbled back, cursing.

She tried to run, but her legs failed her. Weakness settled into her limbs.

Within seconds, her misting ability failed her too, and she began to solidify. Fluffy possessed the same ability, and he was able to utilize it, returning them to their insubstantial state. She tiptoed away, but it was too late. Again, she began to solidify, Fluffy's strength depleted as much as hers. Everyone circled them.

"Go," she commanded Fluffy. "Fetch Br—Cameo." The Forsaken had missed his chance. He'd declined her goods and services. Now, Cameo and her new husband were up to bat. "In Budapest," she added.

The couple currently stayed in the Underworld, where Fluffy couldn't travel. He could only flash places he'd previously visited, and Viola avoided the Underworld at all costs. Too many admirers awaited her. But Fluffy would be safe in Budapest. By the time he figured out the truth, Viola would be victorious or dead.

The trio drew closer, forming a circle around her. Aggression pulsed from them.

"She'll help me." Truth. Cameo would absolutely help...if she could. But she couldn't.

Though frantic, Fluffy obeyed, flashing to Budapest.

Alone with her would-be attackers, Viola clutched her mutilated arm to her chest and grinned. "Shall we proceed?"

One of the vampires grabbed a handful of her hair and forced her to her knees, jostling her. Ripples of agony blurred her vision. Pass out here, now? No! She refused. But though she fought, darkness crept closer and closer.

"Tsk, tsk. You should have been nicer to me," the berserker said with a grin of his own.

As he popped the bones in his hands, the darkness swallowed her whole, and Viola knew nothing more.

Chapter Twelve

Brochan flashed to the fortress in Budapest, exactly as he'd done for the past four days since Viola's disappearance. Just in case. Desperation had become his constant companion. As he moved from room to room, disappointment set in. No sign of his goddess or her friends yet.

He visited the Downfall to question Xerxes. Or Thane. Or Bjorn. Anyone would do. None were there. The world conspired against him.

McCadden remained in the abandoned realm, interrogating anyone Brochan brought to him. Meaning, anyone Viola had spoken to in the past who might know her whereabouts today. He'd gone from one realm to another, visiting all her favorite places and rounding everyone up.

The abandoned realm missed her greatly—and protested mightily. The oasis had already dried up.

Farrow spent the time tracking Forsaken, unwilling to let them find the goddess first. Her dedication remained unwavering.

Brochan braced to flash to a world he had yet to search. Only forty-two others to go. A familiar noise caught his attention, and he paused. His eyes widened. Fluffy? Heart drumming, he appeared in different hallways until he found the devil-dog racing through a bedroom, frantic.

When Viola's pet noticed him, it halted, though awful sounds continued to leave it. Blood splattered its fur, both wet and dry.

Panic infused his every cell. "Where is she?" Brochan turned left, right, shouting, "Viola? Viola!"

The devil-dog spun in circles, the only response Brochan received.

She wasn't here? "Please, take me to her. Let me help her. I *need* to help her." The animal always seemed to understand Viola, obeying her wishes. He prayed the same was true for him. "I'll protect her. This, I swear."

He had hated this creature for so long. Now, he had to rely on its—his—mercy.

"Please," Brochan pleaded.

Fluffy lunged at him, sinking sharp teeth into his calf. Brochan let him, unwilling to harm the—the fortress vanished, a forest surrounding him only a second later. The devil-dog had flashed him?

Relief morphed into alarm when he spotted blood but not Viola. He scented…multiple vampires and a berserker. Males. His claws extended, sharpening as he leaped into motion. He followed the blood.

Fluffy raced ahead of him, taking the lead. If the males had harmed his goddess…

Rage overtook him. *They will pay with their lives.*

Leaves and branches slapped his arms and grazed his wings. His bare feet stomped upon rocks, grinding them into powder.

His ears twitched. Gleeful laughter. Cheers. Eight distinct voices. There! Brochan picked up speed and burst through a wall of thorny foliage.

A group of immortals came into view. Twenty-two individuals, mostly male with only a few females. An assortment of species. The vampires and berserker Brochan had scented before, plus a handful of shifters, warlocks and banshees. They stood in a circle, surrounding something—or someone—too enraptured by whatever was happening in the center of the circle to notice him.

"Not so boastful now, are you?" a banshee called, earning multiple snickers.

Brochan didn't stop to ask questions. He struck. The banshees, the most dangerous beings, dropped first. He slashed his claws through their throats, silencing them before they could scream. As they collapsed, the others noticed him, gearing to attack.

Too late. He swiped with his wings, knocking half the group to the ground—in pieces. To his astonishment, Fluffy fought at his side, preventing a vampire from sneaking up on him.

A pale form capped by twig-tangled blond hair came into view, and Brochan nearly lost it. Viola was on her knees, her arms tied to a stake behind her back. Her head hung low, a gag stuffed into her mouth. Dirt and blood smeared her from head to toe. Her gown remained on her body by only a few threads.

His confident goddess looked…broken.

His knees shook. The urge to go to her assailed him. Resisting tore him apart but resist he did. These people had harmed her. They must suffer.

Vision redlining, he attacked with renewed vigor, slashing through their numbers without mercy. Laughter and snickers became screams. He ensured every blow caused maximum pain and damage.

The last of the immortals ran, bolting for their lives.

"Let them go," Viola seemed to say behind the gag. He must be hearing her incorrectly, because he would have sworn her next words were, "This is deserved."

Brochan shook his head. He didn't want to believe her, but her watery eyes convinced him. She actually requested mercy for her tormentors.

He complied—barely. Though his rage remained high, he flashed to his goddess. His kitten. Tears stung his eyes when he cataloged her injuries. As gently as possible, he freed her from her bonds. Her body sagged against his.

A lump grew in his throat, choking him. "I'm here, kitten. I'm here. Everything is going to be all right." Cupping her cheek, he angled her face toward his.

Feverish eyes glazed with pain struggled to focus on him. With his free hand, he removed the gag. All the while, Fluffy ran circles around them.

"I'm so sorry I didn't remove the cuff. So sorry I pushed you to this."

"No need to save me anymore." Her voice was broken, her words slurred. "No key. Just a rumor. I can't save McCadden. Not the way you hope."

"I'd already begun to suspect. We'll talk about it when you're well." She *would* get well. He refused to accept anything less. He stood as smoothly as possible, doing his best not to jostle her. "Let's go home, yes? Let me take care of you."

"No," she said with a moan, struggling against him despite her weakness. "Won't be imprisoned."

"I'll never make such a mistake again, you have my vow. Please, kitten, do me this honor. You are so precious to me."

"I am?" Her struggles tapered until she sagged against him.

"Come, Fluffy," he said before Viola changed her mind. He flashed to her bedroom. The animal followed.

Brochan stalked into the shower stall. Without releasing his prize, he turned on the water. Blood and dirt swirled down the drain. He didn't bother trying to strip; he sat and propped her against his chest. After removing her dress, he assessed the damage. Her poor stump remained raw and pulpy.

"Always end up in water," she muttered as steam enveloped them. "Makes sense. My mother is Dione. Zeus's first wife."

"The Oceanid and mother of Aphrodite?"

"The very one."

"But she is the goddess who imprisoned you in Tartarus, yes?" The one who'd imprisoned her as a child.

"Mm-hmm. After I escaped her, she accused me of a terrible crime. Had me arrested. And yes, I did kind of murder her servants and destroy her home. If *kind of* means they all died screaming and I left the place in ashes. But I had good reason! My freedom. She feared Zeus learning the truth about her affair with the feline shifter. Not that I remembered that awful, soul-shriveling truth for eons."

"What happened to the memory?"

"The demon. He likes to hide things from me. He especially liked making me believe I had doomed myself with my soul-eating. I guess knowing your mother ruined your life isn't good for your sense of worth. But I digress. My father was..." She groaned. "I can't believe I'm admitting this aloud. He was a lowly...tomcat. He gave me nine lives, at least, each one tied to one of my abilities. He's the reason my godhood revolves around the Afterlife. I used two of those lives to flee her, and three to escape Tartarus. Then I gave one to Fluffy."

The lump in his throat prevented him from speaking, so he kissed her temple instead. She'd been betrayed by a woman who should have loved and protected her. Without friends. No wonder she hated being alone. No wonder she'd chopped off her hand to escape *his* prison. No wonder she clung to her child, the only being who showed her any loyalty.

"I can give one to McCadden too," she offered, desperate. "He'll probably need to feed, just like Fluffy, but he'll live. Or I can help him become a vampire. Whichever you prefer."

His entire being rejected the notion of Viola parting with another life, leaving her only two and depriving her of an ability she required for her safety. "You won't be giving up one of your lives. Promise me."

"No way," she said with more volume.

Rather than argue with her, he said, "Right now, you must concern yourself only with getting better." As he worked to clean the worst of her injuries, he admitted, "I've been inconsolable without you, kitten. Beyond frantic. I searched so many lands. Questioned hundreds of immortals. Not being able to track you…" He shuddered.

"No one can be tracked in the land of the lost." Her words were more and more lucid. "How did you track me before?"

His compliments must be strengthening her. "We'll discuss it later, all right? Right now, I'd like to tell you all the things I admire about you."

"Mmm. Yes. No!" She gave a violent shake of her head. "Discuss how you tracked me *now*."

Though he feared her reaction, he confessed the truth. "The tattoo on my forearm. It's mystically linked to your blood."

Seconds passed in stilted silence as he killed countless excuses for his actions.

"Of all the stalkery things you've done," she finally said, and he mentally prepared for the worst—a demand to leave her. "That might be the best." Did he detect a smile in her tone? He must. A healthy pink flush spread across her skin. "You are utterly *obsessed* with me."

"I am," he said with a nod. "Since the first moment I spied you, I've craved you and no other. There is *no one* better."

Her flush deepened, the skin over her mutilated wrist weaving back together. But only seconds later, the flush faded and the weaving ceased. She shuddered against him. "Those people *hated* me. I'd hurt some of them the same way I hurt you and McCadden. I just…I wanted to save my baby." A sob shook her, tears streaming down her cheeks. "He's my best friend."

"I know, kitten. I know." Brochan rocked her as she cried, his heart breaking. "You are a wonderful mother. The kind I sought for McCadden." *The one I want for my future children.*

Could he win this precious woman when so many others had failed? No, no *could* about it. He would. Because he must. Because he couldn't imagine his life without her. She was the excitement he'd never had. The pleasure he'd always longed to experience. The comfort he hadn't known he needed.

When her tears waned, she sagged against him once more, her eyelids sliding closed. Soon, her breathing evened out. He finished cleaning her, then shut off the water, dried her off and carried her to the bed, where he tucked her in. He should tell his brother and Farrow he'd found her, but he couldn't bring himself to leave. When she woke, he would be here.

Abandon her? Never again.

"Brochan?" she said, her voice slurred once more, fighting sleep.

"Yes, kitten?"

"You are in love with me."

"I…might be," he croaked.

"I must be pretty special then," she said and exhaled slowly, drifting away at last.

He stripped out of his soaked clothing and climbed in beside her, careful of her injuries. Just as carefully, he repositioned her, molding his chest against her back and spreading a wing beneath her. Oh, the rightness of this… How perfectly she fit against him, her body molded to his.

If he had lost her—a roar of denial barreled down his tongue, but he clamped his teeth before the barest sound escaped. Startle her? No.

Fluffy jumped onto the bed and settled in on Viola's other side.

Even in sleep, she sensed the pet's nearness and mumbled nonsense while reaching for him. *The way I want her to reach for me.*

Brochan hadn't slept since her disappearance, but he remained too keyed up to drift off.

He clung to his mate as if she were a lifeline. Perhaps she was. For the first time in his existence, satisfaction danced within his reach. He had his goddess in his arms…but she might demand to leave him when she awoke. Forsaken hunted her for a key she didn't have, and the warriors would never believe the truth.

He must deal with the Forsaken as soon as possible, one way or another. He must win Viola, as well. Could he? Soon, she would give him the test.

He squeezed his eyes shut. Still his mind whirred. And what of Fluffy? The animal would require continued nourishment. He wished he could give the pet his immortality, charging him for the rest of eternity. Although…

An idea struck. What if there was a way? If it failed, Fluffy could die. But if it succeeded…

The beloved "fur-baby" might live forever, no other batteries necessary.

Whatever Brochan did, he couldn't—wouldn't—cut his brother from his life, and that was what Viola would ask of him. He knew it. She expected total adoration, nothing less.

So how could Brochan win her, keep his brother, and save Fluffy?

Chapter Thirteen

Warm and relaxed, Viola stretched. Lights in her mind gradually brightened, and she cracked open her eyelids. Hey! This wasn't the land of the lost. Instead, the master bedroom she'd never thought to see again walled her in. She lay in a soft bed, surrounded by softer wings. Familiar wings. But...surely, he wasn't...

She gulped. Maybe he had. Even breaths caught her attention.

Heart drumming, she craned her neck. Oh, yes. Brochan curled up behind her, one of his legs wedged between her knees. Her eyes widened. Had he ever looked so beautiful? The morning brightness highlighted everything she admired about him: long lashes, freckles, and those mouthwatering horns. They curled back, resting against messy dark hair. He had pointed ears! A delightful trait she hadn't noticed before.

How had—? Memories of his rescue flooded in, and she gasped. *Oh, my.* How positively savage he'd been.

Movement drew her attention to Fluffy, who lay before her with his tummy exposed and all four legs extended in the air. Smiling, she kissed his precious face and maneuvered onto her other side, facing Brochan, only then realizing her hand had regrown.

Another smile broke free as she combed her fingers through her companion's silken hair and toyed with the tip of his ear. He murmured something and leaned into her touch.

I'm winning him, body and soul. He believed he was falling in love with her.

Had he forgiven her for her crimes? Maybe? Possibly? If *he* could pardon her, when he had more reason than most to hate her, shouldn't she pardon herself? She wasn't the girl she used to be. She had confidence now—genuine confidence. The demon had played its best cards, but she'd come out on top.

I will find a way, it growled, its whisper thready.

She rolled her eyes, unimpressed, only to gasp as surprise popped like a balloon inside her head, raining confetti. The fiend was losing its grip on her, weakening while she remained strong.

What a heady realization! She'd have to be careful, though. From experience, she knew how easy it was to slip into old habits and patterns. Which meant she needed to be honest with herself every second of every day. Even the sweetest lie led to bitter regret. So. She would remain aware, always. Test her own motives and intentions. She wouldn't lash out at others in order to feel more powerful. She wouldn't exchange real confidence for the demon's fabricated *over*confidence.

Brochan mumbled her name, and Viola soaked in a haze of warm, wondrous contentment. He might not be the only one falling in love. In the core of her being, she knew they had a chance at happiness here. But...

Would he pass her test?

Tension settled into her bones. Sweat glazed her palms. He was loyal to a fault, yes, but was he loyal enough? She refused to offer her heart to anyone with skewed loyalties. Good intensions were nice and all, but they meant nothing when compared to genuine dependability.

Stomach hollowing, Viola untangled from her companion. She rose, careful not to wake the beasts, both the big and the small. In the bathroom, she brushed her teeth and activated the shower, seeking the comfort of the water. Her most troubling musings followed her. She didn't want to lose Brochan. There was no warrior fiercer, more brilliant, or more beautiful, and she deserved the best. He had to pass her test. He just...had to.

A snarl sounded behind her, startling her. She whipped her head around and gasped. "Brochan."

He loomed in the entrance to the stall, his hands braced on opposite sides of the wall, his naked body leaning in. Any trace of his humanity was gone. His horns stood straight up. Flames had melted his irises. *Like mercury*. Aggression rippled through his wings. The muscles in his abdomen looked as if he smuggled rocks under his blue skin. He pitched his breaths.

He was hard. "I woke up and you were gone. I thought you'd left me again."

A pang rent her chest, and her stomach fluttered. This ferocious male would absolutely pass her test.

Softening, she told him, "I won't leave you without speaking to you first."

"You won't leave me *at all*," he said, his voice like gravel. Wow! The thought of not having her in his life, even for a moment, had wrecked him.

She dipped her gaze over his body. "Is that what you came to tell me?"

"I heard the water and remembered everything I regretted not doing before." He stepped into the stall. A single step.

"Whoa. Hold up." She held out her hands to ward him off. "Before we go any further, we should talk." The test... Best to get it over with.

Concern exploded from him. "Do you still feel sick? Unwell or weak in any way?"

"No. I'm good to go."

"Do you worry Fluffy might see something he shouldn't? Because he left the bedroom at my urging."

"No," she repeated with a shake of her head.

He didn't relax, tension crackling in the air. "Then I don't want to talk. I want to take what's mine."

Okay. All right. That might be the sexiest thing she'd ever heard. Her resistance crumbled. The test could wait. "I'm yours, then?"

"You are. Know this, kitten. You have my pledge of eternal devotion. You are my mate. My wife."

His *wife*? Heavy eyelids sank low as she purred, "Come here, beast."

He needed no further encouragement, stalking toward her. "One day, you'll call me husband."

She...might.

He clasped her waist and half-walked half-carried her to the far side of the stall, where he pressed her against the cool tile and kissed her. As his lips crashed into hers, she wound her arms around him and hooked a leg over his backside.

He kissed her hard, and he kissed her well, *devouring* her. His exquisite taste tantalized her. Though his skin appeared ice-cold, it burned white-hot, searing her to the bone. He kneaded and plumped her breasts as he nibbled the length of her throat.

Soul-shattering bliss. Desperate to give the same, she clasped the base of his ebony horns and stroked up. His spine bowed, his head angling toward the ceiling as he unleashed a mighty roar.

The moment he went silent, he whipped his mouth back to hers, feasting. By the time he next lifted his head, they were both panting.

He pressed his forehead to hers and growled against her lips. "I want to taste you. Slide inside you. Savor. Rush." Claws retracted, he traced a hand over her belly, straight into her slick desire. "I wish to do everything all at once."

Gasps escaped her as he plunged a finger deep. "Brochan!"

"Never felt anything so perfect as you."

Shivers rained over her as surely as the water. Cells flamed, heating the blood in her veins. Limbs trembled. How she ached. Insatiable aches erupted here, there, and there, no part of her unaffected.

She needed...*she needed.* "On your knees. Taste me."

"Yes." He dropped fast, only to pause, stare and slowly run his tongue over his teeth.

And she'd thought him stripped of civility before. No, oh no. This was uncivilized, ravenous hunger etched the lines of his face. "Tell me if I do something wrong."

He'd never done this before? Would he like it? "I guarantee I'll love every second."

With his hands bracketing her waist, he leaned closer, his tongue peeking out...

Lick. Her next gasp tapered into a ragged moan. The rapture!

He moaned. "*Never* take this away from me." Growling, he dove in. Licking. Laving. Thrust, mimicking sex.

Viola lost her mind, thoughts fragmenting. She could only hold on to his horns and rock.

"I'm so close already," she cried. Closer...

Viola shattered with a scream.

His ferocity only intensified. "More!" Brochan dove in again.

Legs about to give out, she flashed him to the bed, flat on his back, his wings flared.

"My turn," she purred.

Their gazes met, his silvery irises ablaze, his breaths ragged.

On her knees, she settled between his legs. She kissed along his abdomen, following a tantalizing happy trail. "Will this be another new experience for you?"

"Yes," he hissed. "Yes. Do it." The agony he evinced... He braced his weight on an elbow and reached out to cup her nape. "Please, wife. Do it."

Wife again. Dizzy with excitement, she licked her lips. "Don't be alarmed when you graduate from thinking you love me to *knowing* it."

Viola licked his length. A hoarse curse exploded from him, his fingers tangling in her hair and flexing. When she sucked him, he released her and fell back, gripping the headboard behind him.

"More," he beseeched.

Always. She brought her hands into play, stroking him as she bobbed.

Incoherent words left him, each coarser than the last. Up, down. Up, down. Faster. Slower. His muscles drew tight.

"Viola! I'm going to… I…won't be able…can't…"

She suckled harder. His back bowed as he came. She reveled in his surrender, growing drunk. At the same time, she'd never felt so empty. The ache inside her proved unbearable.

Shooting up, she fastened her mouth on his. Their tongues twined as he rolled her to her back. With his wings stretched wide, he wedged himself between her thighs, snaked an arm beneath one of her knees and lifted her, creating a cradle for himself.

Yes! His shaft pressed against her opening, and she whimpered.

"Can't get enough of you. Need more," he snarled. "Need *forever.*"

Desperate, she cupped his cheeks, the same way he'd once cupped hers. "Take me, beast. I'm yours."

With a bellow of pleasure-pain, he surged, filling her. Yes! She clutched at him. Her claws sliced his back, sensation pulling her strings.

"Brochan!" Clutching turned to clinging. Here he was, the suitor who'd fought so hard to win her. The warrior who killed for her. The male who prized her.

He pulled out. Plunged back in. Again. Again. Sweat dripped from him. His lips remained stretched over his teeth. Viola lost herself in the throes, every motion fueling the fires of her need. The way he moved, so carnal and possessive.

His big body thrust into hers. Harder. Faster. Blissful friction. Rapturous torment. Beneath him, she writhed and thrashed. Cried out. Pleaded.

He watched her face the entire time, his concentration terrifyingly, gloriously intense. Judging her every reaction to ensure maximum enjoyment?

Undone. "Brochan!" she screamed, a climax detonating.

Guttural sounds left him. A single flap of his wings. His body jerked upright. He held on tight, bringing her with him—remaining buried as she perched on his lap. The next thing she knew, he was hammering into her. He claimed her lips in a brutal kiss. They exchanged breaths and moans, her pleasure rolling on and on.

When she wrenched free to bite the tendon that ran between his neck and shoulder, he threw back his head and bellowed, "Yes, Viola! Yes!" He shuddered against her, his grip bruising. Then they both stilled.

Minutes passed in a suspended reality. They were panting but motionless, trapped in a state somewhere between starved and sated. The time the brain needed to catch up with the stomach.

A smile bloomed. She would feel him later, even when they were apart, and she would know she wasn't alone.

"That was...that..." he stammered. Air seeped from a slit in his lips.

"Mind-blowing. I know." Breathless, boneless, she collapsed on him. Emotions, now untethered, rose and swamped her. Too many to sort through. She only knew she'd never felt so...vulnerable.

This man could break her beyond repair.

He wound his strong arms around her, fusing her against him. "Never letting you go, kitten. Never," he snarled, as if she'd threatened to leave. As she thrilled over his possessive display, he toppled her to the mattress and loomed above her. "I'm going to make you mine again. All day. All night."

To Viola's delight, he kept his word.

Chapter Fourteen

Brochan held an exhausted and sleeping-like-the-dead Viola close. They lay on the bed, her body molded to his. He combed his fingers through her hair and traced the ridges of her spine. He'd lost count of the number of times they'd made love, his need for the little beauty unquenchable. He'd tasted true passion, and he knew—*knew*—he could never live without it again.

All this time, he had considered himself as deathless. The truth was, he'd been a walking corpse until Viola entered the picture. She'd brought him to life. She'd become his mate, his lover, and his lifeline. His only future.

He never had to wonder what she required; she told him. To his goddess, he wasn't a burden to be endured. He was a partner. A prize. *There's no going back now.*

A sense of contentment took up residence deep inside him. This was Nevaeh on Earth. He blinked. A key had always been within his grasp. Only a single decision away: forgive. You couldn't overcome evil with evil, only good. To him, Viola was everything good.

From the darkest of destinies to the brightest of them all. He grinned. Any lingering trace of his bitterness dissolved, gone forever. There was no room for it. He'd had no right to hold on to it, anyway. No right to judge or cast stones. Look at the deeds he himself had committed for lesser reasons. In fighting for the one he loved, he'd become everything he'd once despised.

Viola was right; she deserved better. Too bad for her, she wouldn't get it. She was stuck with Brochan, as he would not be letting her go.

Ever. He didn't think he loved this female; he knew it. He loved her with the whole of his being.

Love, the healer of all wounds.

But what happened if he failed her test?

His body jerked in denial. He couldn't let himself fail. But he couldn't pass, either. What was he going to do?

Sensing his tension, she stirred against him. "Brochan?"

"I'm here, kitten." He kissed her temple, luxuriating as she rubbed against him.

"Good." She blinked open her eyes, all sleepy and soft, and offered him a tender expression. "How much did I rock your world?"

"Impossible to measure," he admitted, and she beamed.

"You've hung around me so long, you've gotten smarter!" Dimming a bit, she nibbled on her bottom lip. "So? Do you want to know how much you rocked *my* world?"

"I already know." His chest swelled with pride. "I clued in when you screamed my name instead of your own."

"That *was* a surprise, wasn't it?" She linked her fingers and rested her chin in the center, directly over his heart. "I mean, I'm the goddess, but you're the one over here working miracles."

The corners of his mouth twitched. He adored this soft, playful side of her. He also adored her full assurance of her power over him. Her confidence fed his.

"What would you like to do today?" he asked.

"Are you taking a day off?"

"I am. We can explore the realm or even remain in bed if we so desire. For the record, I vote we remain in bed."

"Sorry, darling, but this boss babe has a full schedule. Top on the agenda is apologizing to McCadden whether he likes it or not. I'll need your help because I've never actually apologized for anything before and meant it. Also, I'd like to plan my renovation of the palace. We'll take an orgasm break every hour, of course, but this needs to be done if we're going to be ready for our engagement party next week. I mean it. No distracting me more than a few dozen times today. I can't wait to show you off to my acquaintances."

He went still. Everything she'd said hit him with the veracity of a speeding car, all but wiping his brain of all thought. "Every hour? Engaged? Show me off? Me?" The most amazing emotion choked him. She wanted to be with him. Out of every male in every realm, she'd chosen him.

"We are wed, just to be clear," he managed to say.

"Darling, if I married every man who considered himself my husband, I'd be arrested in countless realms. Consider yourself engaged until you pass my test. Besides," she rushed on as he opened his mouth to protest, "we haven't jumped the most essential hurdle. Fluffy must accept you as his father."

She'd called him *darling*. He very much approved of the endearment. "We saved your life together." Without Fluffy, Viola would have died. "He accepts me." And if he didn't, Brochan would work until his claim came true. He owed the baby everything.

Viola rolled her eyes as she oh, so clearly fought a contented smile. "You are so in love with me, it's embarrassing."

Terrifying? World-changing? Yes. Embarrassing? No.

How soon would she insist on issuing her test?

His good humor drained. "Forget lazing about in bed. Let's dress and do something." A distraction would do him some good. Give him time to think and plan. How could he win and lose at the same time?

She gave a mock mournful sigh. "All right, but I think we both know you're only making me do this so you can watch me prance about naked."

Raising his brows, he asked, "Can you blame me?" He would never tire of gazing upon the perfection of all perfections.

"Not in the slightest." Unable to hide a dream-hazed grin, she pressed a hasty kiss to his lips then scrambled from the bed. "You are so lucky you won me."

He gulped. Had he? Won her? That test...

Brochan gripped the sheets and scowled. He couldn't eject the stupid decision from his mind. His entire destiny rested on the results. Pass or fail, fail or pass? If he lost one, he lost everything.

Using his wing joints to push from the bed, he glided directly in front of her, wrapped an arm around her waist and laced a hand through her hair. "Agree you are my wife, kitten." The words were rushed, his urgency unhidden. "There will be no male more devoted than I."

"Believe me, I know," she said, melting into him. "And *you* know what you must do to make your wildest dreams come true and get all this"—she waved a hand to indicate the length of her body—"forever."

Not yet, not yet. Not ready. Sweat beaded over his nape. He wanted her agreement to a union more than anything, and he wanted it now. Needed to bind her to his side in every way imaginable. They were a family now, yes? A rock-solid unit that stayed together, no matter what. Even if a certain someone failed a certain test.

He tightened his hold. "Come. Show me what improvements you'd like me to make on the palace. Your every request is my fervent command."

This pleased her, he could tell. She softened against him, reaching around him to glide her hands over his backside.

Mine! He would win her. He *would.* In the meantime, he prayed Farrow returned with a Forsaken. Brochan's every priority revolved around keeping Viola safe. He could not rest until he laid her enemies at her feet.

Just get through the day. Whatever you do, avoid the test.

"Who are you," she asked, canting her head and nipping his earlobe, "and how long can you stay in Brochan's body?"

Dead serious, he told her, "I am a new man, and I'm *never* going away."

* * * *

"A portrait of me smiling will hang over there." Viola pointed. She and Brochan strolled hand in hand through the foyer. Fluffy trailed behind. "A portrait of me frowning will go there. And there, I'll be scowling. Over the fireplace will be a sketch of us. In it, you'll be smiling, frowning and scowling at the same time. And yes, it's possible. It's all in the eyes."

Brochan muttered a response, clearly not listening to her genius. He was too busy vibrating with aggression and nerves. Well, his distraction was Viola's gain. She ate him up with her gaze, not even trying to hide her leer. He wore his standard apparel: a white T-shirt and black leathers. He looked amazing, blue skin bulging with muscles. His dark hair remained askew, and his horns stood straight. Molten silver eyes whirled with joy, fury, satisfaction and terror.

What bothered him? Why wouldn't he tell her?

Sighing, she led him into a sitting room with dirty sofas and overturned tables. Open balcony doors welcomed sunlight and fresh air scented with roses, the garden right outside. Yes, the oasis and gardens had sprung up anew.

"I don't know if you've met me," she announced, her tone stern, "but ignoring me isn't the way to win me."

"I have a proposition for you," he burst out, as if he'd held on to the words too long. He massaged the back of his neck, growing sheepish. "What if I can keep Fluffy eternally charged without the need for other life? Would you wed me then?"

"Yes!" Viola gripped his arm and jumped up and down. "A thousand times yes!" She would do *anything*. Even postpone her test.

"And what if the procedure... killed him?"

"Oh." She froze, her shoulders wilting. "I'm still intrigued, though. So. Let's hear it. What might save or murder my child."

"*Our* child," he corrected, and she hmphed. "My wings are the source of my deathlessness. Their poison is a part of me, deeply rooted. If we transplanted a root into Fluffy, and it took, he would become like me."

A definite risk with an incredible reward. Dread cut through her excitement. "How would that affect *you*?" She wouldn't risk Brochan. Not even for something as grand as this.

"I will mend. I've had a wing ripped off before, and it grew back."

"But will you be in pain?" she asked, curling into him.

He smiled down at her. "If it works, kitten, I will be in raptures."

Viola flattened her palms against his chest. His heart raced. Their eyes locked. She rose on her tiptoes. He bent his head—

McCadden strode into the room, stopping when he spotted them. He darted his gaze from Brochan to Viola, then back to his brother. With a deep breath, he approached.

As Fluffy jumped between her and the Fallen One, Brochan released her. He severed all contact and cleared his throat. "Has something happened, brother?"

Her stomach twisted. Sensing an opportunity, Narcissism peeked from the shadows of her mind.

Perhaps Brochan is still ashamed of your relationship?

Viola shook her head and squared her shoulders. No! Why go to the darkest place first? Brochan didn't want to hurt his brother, that was all. And she didn't either.

"I'm sorry you helped me ruin your immortal life, McCadden," she blurted out, now that she had the chance. Wait. That had come out wrong. "Let me try again. Don't worry. I can get this right. Because I can do anything." *And...go.* "I regret that I extended your existence for you." No! Bad. How was one supposed to do this, exactly? "I apologize for misleading you? I'm sorry you were hurt by my actions? Yes. Those. But maybe we can extend your life the same way Brochan plans to extend Fluffy's? If you'd like. A wing root," she explained. Was Brochan willing to risk McCadden's life the way she considered risking Fluffy's? "Did you ever consider it?"

"I didn't. I don't think I had the courage to let myself."

"And now?"

"I will allow McCadden to make the decision."

The Fallen One pulled at his collar, drawing their attention. "I'm happy for you, brother," he said. "And I...forgive you, goddess. Mostly. But if you ever hurt my brother, I will—"

"Don't," Brochan interjected with what she assumed was his best impersonation of a *dad voice*. "I love you, lad, but I won't tolerate disrespect to your mother."

She swallowed a snort. See! He wasn't ashamed of her. He'd just claimed her in front of his only son, her former boyfriend.

"Did you refer to me as McCadden's *mother*?" she asked, certain her eyes were twinkling.

He hiked one of his shoulders. "If Fluffy is mine, McCadden is yours."

Crafty Forsaken. He simply hoped to pin her down in every way imaginable, no doubt. Very well. She could play along. Snuggling into Brochan and smiling at the Fallen One, she said, "Feel free to call me Momma. And do yourself a favor. Always remember Momma doesn't like sass."

McCadden looked between them again. "You two deserve each other. You really do." He was mumbling under his breath as he strode off.

Viola snickered, and at first, Brochan joined in her merriment. He deflated right before her eyes and scrubbed a hand over his face. "Brochan?"

Scowling, he motioned to a wall. "Remind me what we're hanging there."

Okay, what was going on? All this because she refused to accept the position of Mrs. Brochan...Something? Well, he knew what he needed to do. Why would he not seek her test to gain his every desire?

There was only one reason. Deep down, he believed he would lose her.

Enough was enough. Viola flashed in front of him and gripped his shoulders, forcing him to stop. Eyes mere slits, she told him, "*Never* tell me I do not do big romantic gestures for you. Because guess what. I'm about to make your wildest dreams come true and...chase you." She shuddered, the words distasteful. Her. Chase a male. "I hope you're happy."

"I'm happier than I've ever been, and I've never been more miserable," he shouted, as if accusing her of another crime. Strain stretched his skin, pulling over muscle. He averted his gaze. More calmly, he told her, "Also, I have no idea what you're talking about."

"The test. Even though you haven't begged me for it, I'm going to give it to you."

Fluffy shrieked and raced from the room as if they'd stripped naked. Kids!

"No." Brochan shook his head. "Don't."

"You're going to win me, Brochan." She grew more certain by the moment. Just look at him.

"But what if I don't?" He clasped her by the waist and yanked her closer. "I can't lose you."

"Then don't." Time to prove she was right, in all ways, always.

Viola melted into him. Using her most official tone, she said, "Brochan the Goddess Tamer, riddle me this. If disowning McCadden forevermore is the only way to be with me, will you do it? And you can't just say you'll do it. You must *do it*, do it. Will you betray your brother to be with me?"

Panting, he dropped his head. His gaze. "Viola...goddess...kitten. Please don't ask this of me. I am begging you."

"Oh, my sweet darling," she said, kissing his chin. "I'm not asking you for an answer. I'm demanding one. Here and now."

He wheezed his next breath, squeezed her waist. "I can't. I just...can't. I'm so sorry. I need you both."

I need you both.

I need you.

I need.

I...

His words echoed inside her head, mini explosions with bursts of fireworks. A brilliant smile bloomed—and yes, she knew it was brilliant because she was Viola. "Congratulations, Brochan! Our party has officially become a reception. You just got yourself a wife!"

His head whipped up, his gaze locking on hers once again. "I passed? But...I don't understand. I refused to part with my loved one. In essence, I rejected you."

"You hush that foul language immediately!" she cried, pressing a hand over his lips. When he merely blinked at her, she lifted her palm.

"You have been so gone for me, you got everything twisted inside your head. The other males *agreed* to betray their loved ones. They switched loyalties easily, never fighting to protect and defend those in their care. If they'll be that way with others, they'll be that way with me, and I had enough of that with my mother."

His mouth opened, closed. Opened, closed. Finally, he said, "Are you saying McCadden betrayed...that he..."

Ouch. Okay, maybe this wasn't the romantic declaration she'd originally envisioned. But truth was truth. "In my future stepson's defense, look at me. Also, I'm certain he regrets it now. And he learned a treasured lesson about how valuable you are to him. Guaranteed he'll never do it again...husband."

"Husband?" A strangled noise escaped Brochan as he sagged into her. "I love you, kitten. I love you so much."

The most sublime contentment filled her, overflowing, all but seeping from her pores.

Narcissism writhed and wailed with agony, as if... Had she closed all doors to him, leaving him without a lair?

She must have! He clawed at her mind; sharp pains left her wincing, but she didn't care. The demon grew weaker... Wait. Her skin was heating. Hotter and hotter. She frowned. Pressure mounted, and alarm surged. What was...why...? Black mist rose from her skin, a cloud forming around her.

"Viola," Brochan rushed out, his fear a match for hers.

Her pain crested. Pain like she'd never known. Radiating. Scorching. Blistering. "Being...torn in...two," she tried to tell him. A scream barreled from her as the mist separated from her completely.

Some internal wound gushed, draining her strength. Her heartbeat slowed... Limbs shook, suddenly boneless. She collapsed.

"Viola!" Why did her new husband sound so...far...

Darkness encompassed her. She fought against it—a bright light flared. Viola gasped and blinked open her eyes. Her pain? Gone. Her mind? Clear.

Brochan held her, terror etched in every inch of his face. Tears wet his eyes.

"What happened?" she asked.

"I think...I think you died," he croaked, hugging her close. "Just for a second. Just long enough to kill *me*."

The mist! It remained in the room, drawing together near the ceiling and coagulating. A grotesque picture soon formed, and she gasped. *Narcissism.* They glared at each other, one foe pitted against the other.

The demon had left her, she realized, ripping out an eternal battery along the way. Killing her. But she had revived.

How long this fiend had tormented her. "You. Are. Grotesque," she said, wrinkling her nose. A hideous creature with bloodred eyes, a skeletal face and a body oozing something putrid. "*Seriously* displeasing to gaze upon."

Brochan followed her line of sight and stiffened. His arm shot out, a sword of fire appearing in his hand. Oh, wow. She'd assumed the Forsaken lost the ability to create those when they fell.

The demon hissed at them and fled, disappearing. And, and, and… "I'm free," she gasped out. The most amazing feeling in the world!

"Yes. You are free, and yet you live," Brochan said, swinging his attention back to her. The sword vanished as he reached for her. "How is this possible?"

"I must have used one of my lives," she explained, then laughed as he spun her around, lifting her feet from the floor. "By the way. I love you, too."

"You love me. Is this truly my life?" When he set her down and pulled back to peer into her eyes and unveil the sweetest, most magnificent smile she'd ever—

Viola sucked in a breath. "No!" She couldn't be seeing what she thought she was.

His smile fell. "What is it? What's wrong?"

"You—Brochan, you have an aura." Acid decimated her throat. "You're soon to die."

Chapter Fifteen

For the whole of his life, no one had ever coddled Brochan. Until now. He loved every second. The only downside...Viola's worry. For days she refused to let him depart the realm or even the palace without her. Which would have been fine with him—he didn't want to be without her for any reason, anyway. Especially since she'd lost her ability to flash.

The cost of her new life.

But. He needed to speak with Xerxes, Thane or Bjorn without an audience. Brochan thought he might be a Sent One again. When the demon had left Viola, he'd sensed the threat to her and reacted on instinct. The sword had simply appeared. The sword he hadn't been able to create since his fall. He hadn't realized the significance at the time, but he had definitely realized it after.

He should be sure before he broke the news to Viola. But, if he *were* a Sent One again, why did he still appear Forsaken? And why couldn't he communicate telepathically with the others? Was he deathless? Would a wing transplant still (possibly) save McCadden and Fluffy?

He and Viola had put the wedding reception on temporary hold, choosing instead to spend their time crafting weapons. Well, she crafted. He observed and guarded.

His goddess labored over a furnace even now, her favorite music blasting in the background. Recordings of her own singing—a true assault to the ears. And yet he reveled in every screeched note.

He wiped the sweat from his brow. Not that it helped. New beads of sweat immediately welled, trickling down his temples. He'd already discarded his shirt and pants. Soon, his underwear would join the pile.

Brochan had turned the royal stables into a royal forge. First, he and Viola had fetched equipment and tools she required, as well as her most prized metals, collected from countless other realms. Fireiron. Bloodgold. Automaton parts. Anything to help him protect himself.

He would cherish whatever she designed for him, but he wasn't worried about dying. Whether he died or not, he would find a way back to her. He'd finally won her. He would not give her up for any reason.

"Fluffy!" McCadden's roar echoed through the forge. His brother stomped inside the blistering room, a pair of boots raised. "Your little monster peed in my shoes. Again!"

The pup rested at Viola's feet, yawning as she hammered at a link.

Brochan stuck out his arm, stopping his brother in his tracks. "Genius is at work. There are to be no interruptions."

"Are you kidding me? First she tells you how she's going to redecorate your home. Now, she has you acting as her doorman." Disgust all but dripped from McCadden. "Is there anything you *won't* do for her?"

"No," Brochan said simply. He derived more joy and satisfaction making his goddess-kitten happy than he'd ever thought possible.

"I have accepted your relationship," his brother continued, growling now. "I'm at a point where I no longer wish to vomit every time I see you together. But I will not tolerate this!"

"And yet you will. I tolerated your tantrums for centuries," Brochan reminded him. "So, you'll learn to live with this." Again and again, he'd wondered if he should tell his brother what he knew. That McCadden had chosen to push Brochan from his life in order to be with Viola. But again and again, he had refrained.

A mistake was made. McCadden had learned from it. Why rub his guilt in his face now? What purpose would it serve? Especially when Brochan had already forgiven him. If his brother had passed Viola's test, Brochan would not have her now.

His gaze found her, as it always did, and he grinned. She'd anchored her mass of hair into a messy bun, sweat making stray strands stick to her cheeks. She wore a pink shirt with a high collar and long sleeves, a pair of gloves, leather pants tucked into steel-toed boots. A leather apron draped her chest, and a tool belt encircled her waist. Safety goggles were perched on her nose.

She'd never looked lovelier.

Contentment enveloped Brochan.

"What's she even making?" McCadden demanded. "No. You know

what? Never mind. I'd rather leave before she notices—"

Viola noticed. She lifted a finger, asking for a moment, and turned down the music. "Hello, son. Momma's busy at the office right now. How about I read you a bedtime story tomorrow night instead?"

A growl rumbled from his brother. "Stop this. I mean it. It's not funny anymore."

"Wow. I give our relationship my all, and this is the thanks I get. Wow," she repeated, clearly affronted. She looked to Brochan. "Kids today, amirite?"

McCadden worked his jaw and muttered, "I dodged a bullet, I really did. She's a terror."

"Yes. She is." Brochan's smile spread wider. "But she's *my* terror."

She blew him a kiss before returning to her task. His heart squeezed. She'd given him Nevaeh on Earth, and he wished to give her something in turn.

What if he could give her Nevaeh, period? Sent Ones' spouses were able to slip past the veil between worlds as easily as Sent Ones themselves. Or at least try? They would find out his origins one way or the other. If the venture proved successful, the Forsaken would be unable to reach her. Threat negated.

McCadden shifted from one side to another, drawing his attention. "You asked me a question the other day," the lad stated softly. "The answer is…I don't know."

Brochan didn't need to rack his brain to recall the question: Did he wish to remain mortal? "When you decide, let me know." He hoped his brother chose a life of immortality. If he couldn't provide a wing root, perhaps McCadden would agree to transition into a vampire, as Viola once suggested. But, if McCadden wished to live and die, for whatever reason, Brochan would respect his choice. What else could he do?

"Brochan, the bracelet is ready," Viola called, removing rubber gloves. "Sorry, I mean the manly *armband*. It's like mine. Now you can behead people the same way I beheaded you. Easily! So, come on and try it out. Oh! And your ring. Impact causes a hook to shoot out. Boom." She punched the air. "You just removed your opponent's eye with a single punch. Really, your options are only limited by your imagination."

He flashed to her, materializing at her side. She currently perched on a stool, bent over a table made of brick. Smiling up at him, she fastened thin links of metal from his elbow to his wrist. The words *Property of Viola* graced each piece.

She showed him how to use it while singing its praises. "Faultless detail. Sharper than any razor. Stronger than any bone."

"It is glorious." The craftsmanship truly awed him.

Chewing on her bottom lip, she perused him from head to toe. Her worry escalated. "I was so certain the bracelet would do the trick, but your aura hasn't improved."

He reached out to smooth the hair from her damp cheek. "Nothing will take me from you, love. I swear it. Not even death."

"Maybe you need more weapons." As she slid an equally masterful ring over his index finger, McCadden closed the distance to look everything over.

His brother whistled. "Should I place my order now or later?"

"Now is fine," she said with a nod. "I'll even give you the friends-and-family discount. Which is full price. But I'll deliver the pieces with a smile. And I won't kill you with them after taking all your money."

"I have captured two Forsaken."

Farrow's voice filled the forge. As Brochan turned to face her, Viola leaped to her feet. Rubber gloves tumbled from her lap.

"I've stored them in the dungeon," the female continued. She looked as if she'd just emerged from a blender. Robe ripped and stained with blood and dirt. Hair wild and windblown. Features pallid and eyes hollow. She didn't spare the goddess a glance. "Come. Let's get this over with." She flashed, vanishing.

Finally! "Let's test your theory about the Forsaken," he said. Would severing their ties to their lifeforces succeed where fire had failed?

"I...no." She shook her head. "I don't want you anywhere near the others. What if they attack?"

He cupped her cheeks. "Remember what I said. I won't be without you." He wasn't Forsaken anymore. He was loved. Stronger, not weaker. "The dungeon is secure. I saw to the repairs myself when I briefly—foolishly—considered keeping you there."

She nodded reluctantly. "Stay here, Fluffy, and guard your brother. He's fragile," she added in a whisper-yell. Then she clasped Brochan's hand and breathed deep. "All right. Let's get this over with."

* * * *

Brochan flashed Viola beneath the palace, where a typical dungeon took shape around them. Dark and dank with stone walls and a dirt floor, the scent of death and despair lingering in the air.

Farrow stood in front of a cell, where two Forsaken paced. Crimson and someone she'd never met. Both males paused when they spotted Viola...and grinned.

Foreboding prickled the back of her neck.

"I told you she'd come," Farrow said—and struck. As she threw her arm in Brochan's direction, a grotesque whip launched from thin air, the handle appearing in her hand. In a blink, hundreds of spiked tentacles wrapped around the man Viola loved. They coiled around his mouth, his neck, his wings, the arms he'd drawn behind his back as he released her, his legs, and bound his ankles together.

The Forsaken yanked, and he tumbled. Viola dove to catch him, ensuring he eased to the floor. Their eyes met, and she had to swallow a cry of distress. His irises blazed with fury, fear and an apology as he struggled against his bonds to no avail. Her worst fear was coming to life.

"Attempt to free him, and he dies. Flash," Farrow said, not knowing the ability was lost, "and he dies. And yes, he will die for good. I lied before and told you the Forsaken had revived from the fire. They didn't. They are nothing but ashes in the wind. Exactly what will happen to Brochan if you fail to give me the key, goddess. Then, I will become your worst nightmare. Because we found a way to ensure we never die again, not even when we die."

Though fear threatened to overtake Viola, she fought to disregard her emotions, good and bad, and straightened. "I don't have a key," she stated flatly. "I never did. I used the rumor to ensure Brochan protected me from the other Forsaken."

"You lie!" the other woman shouted, her eyes glittering with rage.

Speaking of the other Forsaken, they pushed open the door of their cell—one that wasn't locked. Grins widening, they stalked to Viola's side, each clamping one of her arms.

"I'll give you a final opportunity to tell me where you keep the key," Farrow said. "Take Midian to fetch it. I will stay here with Brochan, and Harley will track down your pet and Brochan's brother. I'm sure you've already guessed that they'll die if you return without the key. Trust me, goddess. I've thought about this from every angle. I've planned with painstaking care. Your only hope is cooperation."

Midian—Crimson—leaned down and placed his mouth at her ear. "I'm looking forward to spending some time alone with you, goddess."

Shuddering, Viola closed her eyes. What should she do? What *could* she do? Bluff? Hope Midian teleported her somewhere else, remove his head and hope someone else returned her to the dungeon, praying Brochan wasn't murdered sometime in between? Again, Farrow didn't know he might be a Sent One again and far easier to kill.

It was a risky plan, contingent on many ifs, but it *was* a plan and perhaps Viola's only hope for victory.

Tears threatened to well as she refocused on her foe. Wait. Movement at her left. She whipped to the side, watching as Fluffy zoomed along the corridor. No one else detected him, his body like mist.

"I'll hear your answer now," Farrow snapped.

Viola grinned at her. "My answer is no. Here's why."

Fluffy dove at the other female, sinking his teeth into her neck. Her scream of shock and pain died as the little darling ripped out her throat. She lost her hold on the whip and collapsed, writhing while trying to breathe.

Midian lunged for Fluffy, attempting to rip him off the female. Viola struck, punching her other guard in the temple. Unfortunately for him, she wore a ring with a spring-loaded hook. That hook ejected into his brain and stayed put. As he screamed and yanked at the jewelry he couldn't remove, she swung her other arm, unfastening her bracelet and locking the links in place. The blade sliced through his torso, cutting him in half. But he didn't die. Farrow hadn't lied about finding a way to remain alive when dead.

No matter. He did not fit back together again when his different pieces plopped to the ground, rendering him unable to reach her. On to the next! Farrow still struggled to breathe, Fluffy's fangs still deep in the remnants of her throat. Brochan was using his bracelet to cut through her whip.

Viola concentrated on Crimson. The biggest threat to Brochan's and Fluffy's lives.

The Forsaken stopped pulling and started punching. Screeching, Viola jumped on him, tossing him down. She straddled his waist. As he fought to buck her off, she held on with her thighs and flattened a palm over his heart. Without ceremony, she pushed her spiritual hand from her flesh one, dipping inside him. An ability she hadn't lost.

He jerked, his eyes widening with pain. "What are you doing? Stop!"

"I'll stop...when I'm done." She sank her claws into his spiritual heart and yanked with all her might. Her hand slipped free of his body, a pulsing ball of light filling her palm. Fading...

Just like that, Crimson went still and silent, staring at nothing. Dead for real. A weakness Farrow hadn't foreseen.

"Well, well. Now we know. This works as well as fire." Was he dead for good, though, or would he grow another spiritual heart? Didn't matter, she supposed. Within the hour, she would burn him, too, and ensure her story had a perfect ending.

"Viola!" Panic laced Brochan's voice.

She twisted, finding him partially freed from his bonds and—claws whizzed through the air and scraped through her throat, agony searing her. Like Farrow, she lost the ability to breathe and dropped.

The second Forsaken, Harley, had fully recovered without her knowledge and attacked.

Freeing himself the rest of the way, Brochan dove on the male. With savage, merciless fury, he tore into his opponent, rending him into pieces in a nanosecond.

Spotting a healing Farrow behind him, sneaking closer to attack, Viola tried to scramble over, to warn him, but she had no voice or volume, and she was too far away. The Forsaken reached him first, swiped up the armband sword he'd dropped—the very weapon Viola had gifted to him—and swung.

Rage sparked, only to sizzle out, overcome by shock. She watched, incredulous, as the metal sliced through his neck. His head flew across the corridor, banging into a wall of bars.

He was...

He...

Once again, his body did not possess an aura.

No! He wasn't dead. He *wasn't*. He would heal.

"The key," Farrow grated, stalking toward Viola. "Give it to me."

The rage returned and consumed her. The hottest rage she'd ever entertained. With a violent shove, Viola exited her body. In spirit form, she entered Farrow in a blink, taking over. Possessing the other female utterly and yanking on her reins of control.

"What's happening? What...how...? Get out of me, goddess!" Farrow veered from confusion to astonishment to wrath as she attempted to regain control.

Viola grappled for supremacy to the very end—and won. Cold as ice, she forced Farrow to unsheathe the dagger hanging on her waist.

Viola wasn't the goddess of the Afterlife for nothing.

"Stop this!" The woman struggled to regain the reins of control.

She let the tip of the dagger rest against her carotid and pressed slowly...

"Goddess!"

Did she hear Brochan?

See! He'd lived!

She would speak to him in a moment. She began to saw through flesh, muscle and tendon. Though she and Farrow shared the pain, she did not stop. She kept going until movement became impossible, the head detaching from the body. Then she exited Farrow's motionless form.

Decapitated, and yet the Forsaken remained alive and conscious, as promised. She spewed curses as Viola crawled toward Brochan...who hadn't revived, after all. His head remained unattached, his gaze staring at nothing.

N-no matter. She could fix this. She could. She would, she would, she would. Because she wouldn't give up. Not ever. Panting, wheezing, Viola dragged her male's beautiful head back to his body, doing her best to fit the pieces of the puzzle together.

"Come on! Heal!" He had before.

Like Crimson, he'd just...stopped.

"I'm so sorry, kitten. You were right. Death came for me."

Though she cradled his head in her lap, he spoke from behind her. Or rather, his spirit spoke from behind her.

She knew he petted her hair. She felt a chill, all his warmth gone. Hot tears spilled down her cheeks. "I can fix this."

"You cannot make me a new body, and that is what I need to stay."

Hair slapped her cheeks as she shook her head. "There has to be another way."

Instead of trying to convince her otherwise, he said, "Before I met you, I was the living dead. You brought me to life." His voice cracked at the edges. "I'm not ready to leave you. I'm so sorry," he repeated.

His heartbreak hastened hers, but she shook her head again. "No. No! You're healing, and that's that. I'm the most amazing goddess to ever goddess, and I will not lose my husband."

She got to work, easing his body to the side, scrambling to her feet and issuing commands. "Lie down inside your body without argument. Now."

"I won't let you use one of your lives on me. I can tolerate leaving you only because I know you're safer this way."

"I said now!" she screeched, palace walls shaking. The floor shaking.

Vines shot up from the ground and coiled around his wrists and ankles, even in his spirit form, forcing him to do as she'd commanded. "Thank you," she told the world.

"Viola—"

"You are *not* abandoning me. Not now."

He pressed his lips together. Had he faded even more?

"I'll weld you whole again. Every part of you." She tore off her long-sleeved shirt, revealing the tank top underneath. "I can separate a spirit from a body, so why can't I repair a body and reconnect the spirit?"

Viola worked for hours. With painstaking care, she used streams of her own immortality to sew the intangible into the tangible and connect tangible with tangible. Giving him what he'd forbidden. One of her lives. At some point, Brochan fell into a deep sleep, the vines no longer needed. And still he faded. Faded right before her very eyes.

I won't panic. I won't. Faded wasn't gone. And this was a far more complex surgery than she'd performed on Fluffy when she shared a piece of her heart with him. It was a far more painful surgery, too. In some ways, however, the process was easier. Brochan's body accepted her lifeforce as if they were one and the same. Two halves of a whole. Maybe they were.

If she lost another ability, so be it.

Fluffy remained by her side all the while, primed from battle. At some point, McCadden arrived to gather the pieces of the Forsaken and pile them inside a locked cell for burning later. Or another surgery. Viola's mind raced with possibilities...

Still fading... There was only one Best Mate Ever, and Brochan was it.

Can't lose him. Agony choked her. Tears stung her eyes. Working faster...

Finally, she finished, nothing else to be done. His head was attached to his body, his spirit nestled inside. His eyes remained closed, and she fought for breath, her lungs squeezing. If this failed...

This couldn't fail.

"Brochan." She shook his shoulders. "You wake up right this second. That's an order from your beloved. Wake or I'll be *extremely* cross with you. I might even give you the silent treatment!"

Nothing.

McCadden pulled her head against his chest. Not to stop her but to...comfort her? "He's gone, goddess. He's gone. I am so sorry. I—"

"No!" Too frantic to untangle the meaning behind his actions, she wrenched free and gave Brochan another shake.

"Either you wake up, or I wed your brother-son," she screamed in his face.

His eyelids popped open, rage flaring in his irises. He blinked. "Kitten?"

Relief shoved her into motion. Crying out, she threw herself atop him, and he wrapped his strong arms around her. As she sobbed, he held her and cooed.

When finally she calmed, she sagged against him and sniffled. "I did it. I saved the day."

"You did," he replied. "And you did it well."

"The wellest." Sniff, sniff. He was alive and well, and she was free of the demon. They had hope and a future! "I don't think you'll need a battery charge. You love me so much, I was already a part of you."

Fluffy raced circles around them, clearly excited to have his parents all better.

"Well," she said, "apparently I'm not just the goddess of the Afterlife. I'm the goddess of New Beginnings."

He rolled her to her back, rising above her—to everyone's horror—and brushing the tip of his nose against hers. "We will have the most incredible life together."

"Everyone will be so jealous of us."

McCadden cleared his throat. "Not everyone."

Brochan blinked, satisfaction radiating from him. Then he pressed a swift kiss to Viola's cheek and said, "Babysit your fur-brother, McCadden. Daddy has things to do to Momma." With that, he flashed Viola to their bathroom and stripped her in the shower...

Epilogue

Brochan stood behind Viola, dressed in his *good* leathers. He wasn't wearing a shirt. This way, everyone could admire his deliciousness properly—Viola's words not his. The Wedding Reception-slash-Welcome to Our Realm party had kicked off hours ago, but he and his wife remained at the entrance to the throne room, greeting their guests. Apparently, that was something decent hosts did.

He did no greeting, however; he only grunted. He was too busy admiring his goddess. She wore a sexy pink gown, her pale, glossy hair flowing freely. A smile of joy lit her face as she spoke to her friends and acquaintances, waving families inside the spacious room she'd decorated with endless *couple portraits*.

Fluffy rested in Brochan's arms, hissing at anyone who attempted to pet him.

Brochan kissed his adorable face. "Such a good boy. You make Daddy proud." He and Viola had done as discussed and transplanted a wing root between the animal's shoulders. One of *Farrow's* wing roots.

The procedure had proved easier than expected for both the goddess and their fur-son. Fluffy had rebounded quickly, growing a pair of tiny wings covered in soft down. No more infusions necessary.

"How long must I stand here?" McCadden asked at Brochan's side. A wing root had been offered to him as well, but he had yet to accept. He hadn't rejected the idea either. They had time now. They would figure everything out and ensure a happy ending for everyone.

"Until your mother gives you permission to move," Brochan replied.

His brother scowled. While he remained a Fallen One, Brochan had indeed become a Sent One. Without bitterness, he'd had no poison. Filled with love, he'd healed. In the process, he had retained his physical form.

What strength you gained through experience, you kept.

Viola motioned him closer, saying to a pretty brunette, "This is the stalker I texted you about. Isn't he divine?" She leaned her head against his shoulder. "Brochan, this is my on-again off-again friend, Cameo, former keeper of the demon of Misery. We're currently on again, since she started texting me again."

His chest swelled with pride. He loved when his goddess claimed him. "I am her husband now," he said.

The brunette responded to him, then seemed to say something teasing to Viola, but he didn't hear her actual words. Viola was beaming at him. He only heard the sound of joy.

"Viola!" a young boy with a mop of black hair and vivid violet eyes bellowed. He marched over, a lad on a mission, brushing past the one named Cameo, only to stop abruptly and bow. "Goddess. I'm not supposed to say this because it's supposedly creepy, but I missed you and you are beautiful and I'm going to marry you one day."

Brochan stiffened. Um…what now?

"Urban," she twittered. "How wonderful to see you, darling. Brochan, did I ever delight you with stories about how I saved the Lords of the Underworld and their children? Remind me to tell you all the details later. Anyway, I babysat Urban, and he developed a bit of a crush. Naturally." Leaning down, she said to the boy, "I have a fantastic surprise for you. A new obsession, in fact."

Straightening, she motioned to the wall behind them, positioned between two flights of stairs, where Farrow's head hung, mounted like a prized deer…but still alive. And still without a body.

"She's beautiful, isn't she?" Viola asked.

The kid peered up at Farrow and shrugged. "Yeah. So?"

"She's also selfish?" Viola seemed to ask a question while stating a fact.

Again, the boy shrugged.

"She's very…naughty?" Again, the goddess seemed to ask a question.

Now little Urban perked up. He gave Farrow another look, this one lingering, soon becoming admiring. Even adoring. Well, well. He'd taken the bait. Although…

"I don't know if I'm insulted or not," Viola mumbled to Brochan. "I thought he liked me for my exquisite face. Turns out, he has the hots for the baddest girl to ever bad."

"I have the hots for the hottest girl to ever hot," Brochan told her, earning a smile.

The line of guests moved along, finally tapering off.

Brochan and Viola loomed outside the throne room. He sat Fluffy down and wrapped his arms around his mate. She'd given up so much to be with him. To heal him, she'd lost her ability to mist, one of her greatest defenses. Brochan was determined to always guard her. Though he doubted anyone would ever dare try to harm her again.

Word had spread. Viola could kill the unkillable.

"We have the best story," she said, beaming up at him. "The world's most perfect goddess meets a hardened soldier with a grudge, who teaches her something for reasons before she snags his heart."

The whiskey irises he so adored glittered at him. He kissed the smile teasing her lips. "Never change."

"Never." A solemn vow. Then she kissed the smile on his lips. "I'm feeling extra braggy about you today, so be my darling and tolerate the crowd for a solid five minutes. *Then* you can shout at everyone to leave, and I'll give you a horn job." With a wink, she sauntered away.

Horns suddenly ramrod straight, he stomped after her. He'd give her three minutes. Possibly two. Or one. Or none.

"Get out! Out of my palace!"

* * * *

Also from 1001 Dark Nights and Gena Showalter, discover The Darkest Assassin and The Darkest Captive.

Sign up for the 1001 Dark Nights Newsletter
and be entered to win a Tiffany Key necklace.

There's a contest every month!

Go to www.1001DarkNights.com to subscribe.

**As a bonus, all subscribers can download
FIVE FREE exclusive books!**

Discover 1001 Dark Nights Collection Eight

DRAGON REVEALED by Donna Grant
A Dragon Kings Novella

CAPTURED IN INK by Carrie Ann Ryan
A Montgomery Ink: Boulder Novella

SECURING JANE by Susan Stoker
A SEAL of Protection: Legacy Series Novella

WILD WIND by Kristen Ashley
A Chaos Novella

DARE TO TEASE by Carly Phillips
A Dare Nation Novella

VAMPIRE by Rebecca Zanetti
A Dark Protectors/Rebels Novella

MAFIA KING by Rachel Van Dyken
A Mafia Royals Novella

THE GRAVEDIGGER'S SON by Darynda Jones
A Charley Davidson Novella

FINALE by Skye Warren
A North Security Novella

MEMORIES OF YOU by J. Kenner
A Stark Securities Novella

SLAYED BY DARKNESS by Alexandra Ivy
A Guardians of Eternity Novella

TREASURED by Lexi Blake
A Masters and Mercenaries Novella

THE DAREDEVIL by Dylan Allen
A Rivers Wilde Novella

BOND OF DESTINY by Larissa Ione
A Demonica Novella

THE CLOSE-UP by Kennedy Ryan
A Hollywood Renaissance Novella

MORE THAN POSSESS YOU by Shayla Black
A More Than Words Novella

HAUNTED HOUSE by Heather Graham
A Krewe of Hunters Novella

MAN FOR ME by Laurelin Paige
A Man In Charge Novella

THE RHYTHM METHOD by Kylie Scott
A Stage Dive Novella

JONAH BENNETT by Tijan
A Bennett Mafia Novella

CHANGE WITH ME by Kristen Proby
A With Me In Seattle Novella

THE DARKEST DESTINY by Gena Showalter
A Lords of the Underworld Novella

Also from Blue Box Press

THE LAST TIARA by M.J. Rose

THE CROWN OF GILDED BONES by Jennifer L. Armentrout
A Blood and Ash Novel

THE MISSING SISTER by Lucinda Riley

THE END OF FOREVER by Steve Berry and M.J. Rose
A Cassiopeia Vitt Adventure

THE STEAL by C. W. Gortner and M.J. Rose

CHASING SERENITY by Kristen Ashley
A River Rain Novel

A SHADOW IN THE EMBER by Jennifer L. Armentrout
A Flesh and Fire Novel

Discover More Gena Showalter

The Darkest Assassin: A Lords of the Underworld Novella

Fox is a demon-possessed immortal with many talents.
--Ability to open portals—check
--Power to kill the most dangerous Sent Ones—check
--Scare away any man who might want to date her—mate
Now, the keeper of Distrust has been marked for death, a winged assassin with rainbow-colored eyes tracking her every move, determined to avenge the males she accidentally decimated. If only she could control the desire to rip off his clothes…

Bjorn is a fierce warrior with many complications.
--Tragic, torture-filled past—check
--A wife he was forced to wed, who is draining his life force—check
--Ever-intensifying desire for the enigmatic Fox—mate
Never has he hesitated to exterminate an evil being. Until now. The sharp-tongued female with a shockingly vulnerable heart tempts him in ways no one else ever has, threatening his iron control.

But, as Fate itself seems to conspire against the unlikely pair, both old and new enemies emerge. And Fox and Bjorn must fight to survive.

And learn to love…

* * * *

The Darkest Captive: A Lords of the Underworld Novella

For centuries, Galen the Treacherous has been the most hated immortal in the Underworld. With good reason! This bad boy of bad boys has lied, stolen, cheated and killed with abandon. Possessed by the demons of Jealousy and False Hope, he has always lived for a single purpose: destroy *everything*.

Then he met *her*.

Former demon turned human femme fatale — Legion Honey --
sought to kill Galen, but ended up parting with her virginity instead.
Afraid of their sizzling connection, she ran away…and ended up trapped
in hell, tortured and abused in the worst of ways. Now she's free, and a
shell of herself, afraid of her own shadow.

Galen's hunger for Legion has only grown. Now the warrior with
nothing to lose must help her rekindle the fire that once burned inside
her. But as desires blaze white-hot, will Legion run again? Or will the
unlikely pair succumb to love at long last?

The Darkest Assassin

A Lords of the Underworld Novella
Now available!

Fox pressed a series of tiles on the wall before rushing out of the shower stall. Ahead, a section of the wall popped open, revealing a sword hilt. As soon as she reached it, she grabbed that hilt, freeing the weapon. A little compartment she'd built for emergencies like this. She refused to open a portal to a new location. Her attacker(s) might or might not follow her through. If not, Galen and Legion would be vulnerable to ambush. No, Fox would stay, and she would fight.

As she rounded the corner, she spied golden feathers. Oh, yes. A Sent One had come for her. Though she'd locked up her emotions, a new one sparked. Awed terror. This wasn't just any Sent One. This was one of the Elite 7. The best of the best for allies, the worst of the worst for enemies.

Suddenly, she came face-to-face with the most beautiful male of all time. Dark hair, bronzed skin. Rainbow eyes. Wow, wow, wow. His irises contained hints of blue, green, gold, and red.

The terror faded, leaving only awe. He wore a long white robe and held a sword of flames. How he'd gotten past her friends, Fox didn't know. Surely, someone had heard his entrance.

If so, she had a minute, perhaps two, before that someone showed up to check on her. Unless the Sent One did something to prevent others from hearing what occurred in her room. Or killed those others.

Rage overwhelmed her. "Did you hurt my friends?" The question exploded from her.

"I did not."

The rage dulled, and their gazes met, awareness punching her dead center in the chest. Never in all the eons of her life had she experienced such a visceral reaction to another person.

As she struggled to take in air, he pursued her inch by inch. He liked what he saw, no doubt about it. An erection tented his robe an-n-nd damn! He couldn't be that large. Nope. No way. He must have smuggled in a package of tube socks filled with dildos. Either way, her nipples puckered and goose bumps spread over her limbs.

He swallowed. "You are Fox the Executioner." A statement, not a question, spoken in a delicious, gravelly voice.

New shivers hurried down her spine. "I am." Why deny it?

"Then you know why I'm here."

"I do." Again, there was no reason to deny it. "Nice hate-on, by the way."

A growl rumbled from him.

Excellent. She pushed back a little more. "Be honest. You're regretting your assignment now that you've seen me, yes? I mean, it's pretty obvious you gave my body a five-boner review." Despite the dire circumstances, Fox couldn't help but tease the big, bad warrior who'd come to slay her...a male who looked like sex on legs and sounded like the world's best-paid phone sex operator.

A blush painted twin circles of pink on his cheeks.

A blush? From an assassin? How adorable was that? Even still, she lifted her blade. As much as she'd struggled to survive her childhood, as fiercely as she'd fought to endure her demon, she would not go down without a fight. No matter how much she deserved the punishment.

"You are mistaken. I regret nothing," he told her. "An involuntary bodily reaction *changes* nothing."

"Or maybe it changes everything. Who are you, anyway?" And why hadn't he launched his first strike, if he had no regrets?

"I am Bjorn, the One True Dread."

Well, well. He'd actually answered.

About Gena Showalter

Gena Showalter is the *New York Times* and *USA TODAY* bestselling author of the spellbinding Lords of the Underworld, Rise of the Warlords, and Immortal Enemies series, as well as three young adult series—The Forest of Good and Evil, Everlife and the White Rabbit Chronicles—and the highly anticipated Jane Ladling Mystery series, cowritten with Jill Monroe.

She's hard at work on her next novel, a tale featuring an alpha male with a dark side and the strong woman who brings him to his knees. Check her website often to learn more about Gena, her menagerie of rescue animals, and all her upcoming books. https://genashowalter.com

Discover 1001 Dark Nights

Paige ~ CLOSER by Kylie Scott ~ SOMETHING JUST LIKE THIS by Jennifer Probst ~ BLOOD NIGHT by Heather Graham ~ TWIST OF FATE by Jill Shalvis ~ MORE THAN PLEASURE YOU by Shayla Black ~ WONDER WITH ME by Kristen Proby ~ THE DARKEST ASSASSIN by Gena Showalter

COLLECTION SEVEN

THE BISHOP by Skye Warren ~ TAKEN WITH YOU by Carrie Ann Ryan ~ DRAGON LOST by Donna Grant ~ SEXY LOVE by Carly Phillips ~ PROVOKE by Rachel Van Dyken ~ RAFE by Sawyer Bennett ~ THE NAUGHTY PRINCESS by Claire Contreras ~ THE GRAVEYARD SHIFT by Darynda Jones ~ CHARMED by Lexi Blake ~ SACRIFICE OF DARKNESS by Alexandra Ivy ~ THE QUEEN by Jen Armentrout ~ BEGIN AGAIN by Jennifer Probst ~ VIXEN by Rebecca Zanetti ~ SLASH by Laurelin Paige ~ THE DEAD HEAT OF SUMMER by Heather Graham ~ WILD FIRE by Kristen Ashley ~ MORE THAN PROTECT YOU by Shayla Black ~ LOVE SONG by Kylie Scott ~ CHERISH ME by J. Kenner ~ SHINE WITH ME by Kristen Proby

Discover Blue Box Press

TAME ME by J. Kenner ~ TEMPT ME by J. Kenner ~ DAMIEN by J. Kenner ~ TEASE ME by J. Kenner ~ REAPER by Larissa Ione ~ THE SURRENDER GATE by Christopher Rice ~ SERVICING THE TARGET by Cherise Sinclair ~ THE LAKE OF LEARNING by Steve Berry and M.J. Rose ~ THE MUSEUM OF MYSTERIES by Steve Berry and M.J. Rose ~ TEASE ME by J. Kenner ~ FROM BLOOD AND ASH by Jennifer L. Armentrout ~ QUEEN MOVE by Kennedy Ryan ~ THE HOUSE OF LONG AGO by Steve Berry and M.J. Rose ~ THE BUTTERFLY ROOM by Lucinda Riley ~ A KINGDOM OF FLESH AND FIRE by Jennifer L. Armentrout